108課綱、全民英檢中級適用

英語 *Make Me High* 系列

You Can Write !

寫作導引

李文玲 編著

英語 Make Me High 系列

You Can Write! 寫作導引

編 著 者	李文玲
發 行 人	劉振強
出 版 者	三民書局股份有限公司
地　　址	臺北市復興北路 386 號 (復北門市)
	臺北市重慶南路一段 61 號 (重南門市)
電　　話	(02)25006600
網　　址	三民網路書店 https://www.sanmin.com.tw
出版日期	初版一刷 2003 年 4 月
	初版四刷 2006 年 7 月
	修訂二版一刷 2007 年 9 月
	修訂二版七刷 2021 年 5 月
書籍編號	S804380
	4712780660980

三民書局

序

英語 Make Me High 系列的理想在於超越，在於創新。

這是時代的精神，也是我們出版的動力；

這是教育的目的，也是我們進步的執著。

針對英語的全球化與未來的升學趨勢，

我們設計了一系列適合普高、技高學生的英語學習書籍。

面對英語，不會徬徨不再迷惘，學習的心徹底沸騰，

心情好 High！

實戰模擬，掌握先機知己知彼，百戰不殆決勝未來，

分數更 High！

選擇優質的英語學習書籍，才能激發學習的強烈動機；

興趣盎然便不會畏懼艱難，自信心要自己大聲說出來。

本書如良師指引循循善誘，如益友相互鼓勵攜手成長。

展書輕閱，你將發現……

學習英語原來也可以這麼 High！

改版序

　　本書於 2003 年出版，作者經過三年的觀察後，決定著手在書中加入更符合時宜的練習和範文，希望藉此引發更多莘莘學子的學習興趣。修改的主要部份是：

一、練習題全新設計，由淺入深，由易而難，也更符合大考趨勢。例如第 4 頁參考學科能力測驗設計的連環圖畫。

二、大幅更新範文，更符合社會現狀或學生生活，進而引起讀者更高的學習興趣。例如第 58 頁網路受害者、第 71 頁部落格的問題和第 85 頁學校舞會的事件。

三、調整部份架構，更具有層次，使讀者能一目了然。例如第三章第 38 頁先列出學生常犯的錯誤，然後說明造成錯誤的原因並提出如何修改的範例。

　　當然這本書還是保留了原有受好評的架構與精神，可以循序漸進帶領你：

一、從寫作前的構思活動中找尋靈感與文思，並將文思組織起來。

二、認識段落結構，並藉由引導式的活動，學習如何寫主題句、支持句與結論句。

三、加強你對統一性和連貫性的概念，學會避免偏離主題與邏輯不清。

四、具備基本寫作概念後，在第四章練習九種作文練習，奠定好你能寫出大約 120 字左右段落文章的能力。

五、在第五章中更上一層樓，不管你要參加學科能力測驗，或者英檢、托福、GRE 的考試，這一章可以幫助你作文更加精進。

六、在第六章和第七章中介紹摘要與私人信函的寫作方式，提供更實際的應用。

七、在每一章之後的 Teacher's Note 單元，更與讀者分享一些寫作的小技巧，與寫作時常犯的錯誤。

　　本書除了提供普高和技高的學生培養作文能力，為考試作準備之外，也非常適合非英語系的大學生或社會人士自修，以增進作文能力或參加各類考試。

Y O U C A N W R I T E

寫作導引

▶▶ CONTENTS

Step into Writing

Pre-writing and Outlining
構思活動與製作大綱

▶ 是否有過這種經驗呢?盯著作文題目看卻找不到靈感,無法構思。本書第一章就要介紹幾個尋找文思的方法。

寫前構思
Pre-writing

　　寫前構思是指從看到題目到正式下筆寫作文之間尋找文思的過程。可以藉由腦力激盪的活動從大腦記憶中找出資料,進而篩選成為真正可用來寫作的材料。通常五十分鐘的作文課,寫前構思大概可以花六、七分鐘。這些腦力激盪的活動可以是個人的活動,也可以由老師設計來做為作文課的班級活動。

　　以下要介紹的四種構思活動分別是問問題 (asking questions)、畫構思圖 (clustering)、列出與分類 (listing and grouping) 和隨想隨寫 (freewriting)。在寫作文時可以依照題目的性質、作文的時間或自己的喜好選擇不同的方法。

問問題
1a-1 Asking Questions

　　針對題目以提出問題的方式來尋找文思。這些問題都是以 Who、Where、When、What、Why、How 這些疑問詞開始的問句。

　　以 95 年度學科能力測驗作文三張連環圖畫為例,提出問句會是很不錯的構思方法,幫助你想出要寫些什麼來完整地敘述圖中所發生的事件。

- Where were the lady and the dog?　• What was the lady doing?
- Why was the dog waiting there?
- How did the gorilla get into the kitchen? Silently or noisily?
- Why did the lady get startled?　• What were scattered on the floor?
- What was the dog doing?　• How did the gorilla turn into a gentleman?
- Who was the gentleman?　• Why did the lady look so happy?

提出問題對於敘述故事是很有幫助的構思活動。

Activity 1

仔細看看下列的連環圖畫，練習提出問句的構思方法。

1a-2 *Clustering* 畫構思圖

　　畫構思圖就是依著主題自由聯想，畫出文思發展圖，從中選擇適合的文思發展方向。例如房間裡有好幾樣珍貴的東西，而你不知道要介紹哪一樣，就可以用這個方法。以 **Something Precious in My Room** 這個主題做自由聯想，找出最適合你寫的題材：

step 4

‧最後就可以清楚地看出哪一串有最多的細節可寫，或者最能吸引讀者，就是最合適的題材。

step 3

‧看看還有什麼細節 (detail) 可以像蜘蛛結網一樣一層一層畫下去，直到無法再聯想。

step 2

‧先把聯想到的東西畫在框框的四周。(如下圖紅色圈圈)

step 1

‧先在白紙的中間寫主題 (something precious in my room)，然後圈起來。

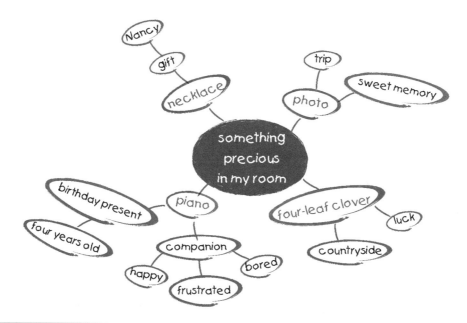

Activity 2

請以 **Cell Phones** 這個題目自由聯想，畫出你自己的構思圖。

1a-3 Listing and Grouping
列出與分類

這個方法是盡量發揮聯想力，列出所有大腦裡庫存的資料，然後經過分類篩選的過程找到可用的材料。以「都市生活」這主題為例：

Step 1: 盡量去想，把所有想得到有關大都市的優缺點都列出來。

Step 2: 把列出的項目歸類之後，給每一個類別一個關鍵字或片語 (key word or phrase)。

Step 3: 然後依照篇幅或重要性，取捨與篩選出適合的寫作文的材料。

Benefits		**Drawbacks**	
many resources	stores	high crime rate	dirty air
public transportation	film theaters	noise	heavy traffic
museums	concert halls	stress	dense population
job opportunities	health care		

在做這些活動時，你要做的就是盡量腦力激盪，拼字或文法都不重要。

Activity 3

假如你要向外國人說明中國人的迷信，或者是老師要你寫一篇作文，題目是 **Superstitions in Chinese Culture**。先腦力激盪一番，模仿上面的例子，把能想到的迷信全列出來，再分類整理。看看你可以分成幾方面來說明。

1a-4 *Freewriting* 隨想隨寫

　　隨想隨寫也是利用自由聯想來發揮文思。方法是：
- 盡量去聯想與主題相關的人、事或物，連續寫三到五分鐘。
- 不需顧慮拼字與文法的正確性。
- 如此腦力激盪之後，重讀一次，篩選出適合的文思。以下是一個隨想隨寫的例子 (其中包括不適當的用字及文法)：

> ### The Use of Animals in Medical Research
> *The use of animals in medical research has many practical benefits. When researchers in the laboratory want to determine the effects of a new medicine, animals are the best testing subjects. Some animals like monkeys、白老鼠 react to medicine in almost the same way as us. This way we can ensure the safety. Human beings don't have to risk losing valuable lives just for testing new medicine. Abandoned animals that stray on the streets are a big problem these days. Medical research is an excellent way to solve the problem. I don't think using animals in research is cruel.*

1b *Outlining* 製作大綱

   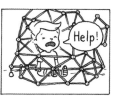

　　找到寫作材料之後，下一步就是製作大綱，把這些材料有效地組織起來。

1b-1 大綱的功能

大綱 (outline) 有助於將要點和細節組織得有條有理，以及合乎邏輯次序，大綱架構出來後，作文的結構才能嚴謹而有條理。

1b-2 大綱的形式

比較常用的是要點大綱，也就是用單字或片語，而不用完整的句子寫大綱。

1b-3 製作的方法

- 以 1a-3 的例子為例，有兩項要點：benefits and drawbacks。要點的安排可以先談優點後談缺點，或先談缺點後談優點。
- 再加上細節部分就成了段落主體部分的大綱。
- 進入第二章之後，學會了寫主題句和結論句，就可以寫出完整的段落大綱。

 範例

Topic Sentence: Life in big cities has its benefits and drawbacks.
Body:
1. benefits
    a. convenience—stores, public transportation
    b. cultural activities—museums, concert halls, film theaters, colleges
    c. better health care—hospitals
2. drawbacks
    a. social problems—high crime rate
    b. pollution problems—litter, noise, dirty air
    c. stress
Concluding Sentence: People have both positive and negative view of city life.

Activity 1

　　根據你在 1a-2 的 Activity 2 所畫的構思圖,找出你要寫的題材並將細節整理好之後,請擬出大綱來。

Activity 2

　　以 **My Favorite Family Member/Holiday** 為題,先做構思活動,之後再擬出大綱。

1b-4 文章的大綱模式

　　以下屬於 Essay 寫作的範圍,可以和第五章 Essay Writing 配合著學!

　　文章大綱除了引言當中最重要的主旨陳述 (thesis statement) 以及結論當中足以涵蓋整篇文章的結論句 (concluding sentence) 之外,主體部分就是由數個段落大綱組成的。

Title: City Life and Country Life

I. Introduction

　　1. City life and country life are two different things.

　　2. People's views of city life or country life may be either positive or negative.

II. Body

　　1. Benefits of living in a big city

a. convenience

b. cultural activities

c. better health care

2. Drawbacks of living in a big city

a. social problems

b. pollution problems

c. stress

3. Benefits of living in the country

a. slow pace of life

b. fewer pollution problems

c. getting close to nature

4. Drawbacks of living in the country

a. inconvenience

b. fewer job opportunities

III. Conclusion

1. Both city life and country life have positive and negative aspects associated with them.

2. Choosing where to live is often not so much of a choice but rather an act of necessity.

■ 構思和寫大綱很重要嗎？這些構思活動在考試的時候可以用得上嗎？

　　作文要能層次分明、結構嚴謹，寫作之前就要有規劃。構思和擬定大綱就是寫作規劃，所以很重要。有人看到題目，毫不思索，提筆就寫。這樣寫作文常常會導致沒有條理、結構鬆散或者無法節制、離題太遠。

　　如果平時練習寫作文時能多練習這些腦力激盪的活動，考試的時候你就可以快速而且靈活的運用。也就是說，考試時你不必規規矩矩的寫下那些問題、記下要點或畫出整齊的圖。問題在你自己腦中，圖你自己看懂就好。

　　有一位參加 91 年度學科能力測驗的考生，她就做了這樣的構思活動。作文題目是 **The Most Precious Thing in My Room**。她的寫作步驟是：

1. 審題：
   確定這篇作文的重點是「這件東西為何珍貴」，也就是要描述物與我之間的情感關係。
2. 畫構思圖：
   因為當時腦子裡閃現了四樣同樣珍貴的東西，因此利用試題卷空白處畫了構思圖，就是 1a-2 Clustering 部分的範例，選擇了 piano 這個比較可以發揮的題材來寫。
3. 依照此圖擬好了簡單的要點大綱：
   Point 1: a friend to be with when I feel bored
   Point 2: a friend to share joy when I am happy
   Point 3: a friend to help heal my sorrows when I am feeling down
   其中把最重要的放在最後一項。另外因為要點並沒有太多的細節要寫，所以決定只寫一段。
4. 想好主題句。

　　徵得這位同學同意後，取得這篇作文，也尊重她不具名的要求。我們來看看她得了 18 分的作文是怎麼寫的！

The Most Precious Thing in My Room

—— 主題句

The most precious thing in my room is the huge brown piano, which my mother bought for my birthday when I was only four years old. It has been my companion for more than 13 years. Whenever I am extremely bored, without anything else to do, I just sit at my piano. Amazingly, there must be some melody that comes into my mind as soon as my fingers touch the keys. My piano seems to be playing fun games with me. When I win some prizes, get good grades, or have a wonderful day with my friends, I can't wait to go back home to tell my piano everything that makes me happy. It is always the one with whom I share my joy. But, what makes me appreciate it most is that it helps to heal all my sorrows. Playing the piano especially when I am feeling down is particularly therapeutic. Every time I feel terribly frustrated as if it's the end of the world, I just close the door, lock myself in my room, and open my heart to the piano. Only through my dancing fingertips on the keyboard can I release my pent-up emotions. It seems that I always confide everything to my piano. The huge brown thing has become an intimate friend I can trust and the most precious thing in my room.

■要怎麼決定用哪一種構思方法呢？

　　通常你要從好幾個主題當中選擇一個的時候，畫構思圖 (clustering) 就比較適合。例如要寫一個讓你可以放鬆心情的地方 (A Place to Relax)，你很可能要由幾個地方當中選擇，這時就可以畫構思圖，從中找出一個地方是有最多細節可以發展的。

　　有人認為問問題是最簡單的方法，但是先決條件是你要知道問什麼問題，也就是你必須先要審題正確，清楚哪些問題的答案是組成這篇作文所需要的。當然這是多練習之後就能學會的。

　　另外你要分項說明時，就像 1a-3 的 Activity 3 要介紹中國人的迷信，或者要討論原因或結果、相同點或相異點，你需要先想出細節再整合時，列出分類就很適合了。

The Structure of a Paragraph
段落的結構

▶ 段落是由一群彼此有關聯、表達一個中心思想的句子組成的。進入正式的段落寫作前，我們先來認識段落的結構。

2a

段落的組成
The Composition of a Paragraph

　　英文寫作的段落通常有三個部分：由段落開頭的主題句陳述本段的主旨，然後再用一些支持句來闡述主題句，最後以結論句來總結。

· 主題句 (topic sentence)——它的功能除了清楚地告訴讀者本段的主旨，還可以指引或約束作者自己段落擴展的方向。初學寫作者最好把主題句放在段落的第一句或第二句。

· 支持句 (supporting sentences)——此為段落的主體，應運用各種技巧清楚而完整地針對段落的主旨進行闡述或論證。

· 結論句 (concluding sentence)——通常在段落結尾處，將段落內容做個歸納或總結，若觀點論述很完整時這部分是可以省略的。

這三部分的比例要適當，支持句部分佔的比例最大，以能夠充分發展主題句為原則。

　　以下是有完整結構的段落範例：

範例

—— 主題句

　　Children's encounters with poetry should include three types of response—enjoyment, exploration, and deepening understanding. Children must start with enjoyment, which helps them keep holding their interest in poetry. When they find delight in the poems, they are ready and eager to explore further. They try to see implications beyond the obvious to read for hidden meanings. This is reading for deeper understanding, taking a thoughtful look at what lies beneath the surface. Enjoyment, exploration, and deeper understanding must all be part of children's experience with poetry.　結論句　（改寫自 93 年度指考考題）

說明 第二句以後的支持句很詳細的說明了 **three types of response** 之間的相互關係：喜歡詩 (start with enjoyment)，進一步探索詩 (eager to explore)，瞭解詩中隱含的意義 (read for hidden meanings)。

Topic Sentences 主題句

2b-1 主題句的構成

　　主題句包含兩個部分：

主題 (**topic**)——要談論的議題。

主題論述 (**controlling idea**)——對議題提出看法，目的是限制主題討論的範圍，以主導段落發展的要點，讓讀者一讀便知要談論什麼。

例如要寫一段有關電腦的段落，topic 為 computer。若是想談論電腦對生活的影響，其 controlling idea 可以是 "make our lives easier and more convenient"。因此主題句就是：

　　　　Computers make our lives easier and more convenient.
　　　　　主題　　　　　　　　　　　　主題論述

Activity 1

　　以下有四句主題句，用括弧括出 topic，並將 controlling idea 部分畫底線，第一題為範例。

(1) To (dance well), you need to have a good sense of rhythm.

(2) Idioms can reveal some aspects of the culture behind a language.

(3) Bats perform an important ecological function throughout the world.

(4) It is easy to form bad eating habits.

(5) Nutritionists have made several recommendations to help teenagers control their weight.

2b-2 寫主題句時應注意的事項

- **主題句必須是完整的句子 (sentence) 而非片段 (fragment)**

  Learning English → 片段

  Learning English is important to me. → 完整的句子

  If I had magical power → 片段

  If I had magical power, I would turn the world into the one full of love and peace. → 完整的句子

- **主題句必須語意清楚 (clear) 而不模糊 (not vague)**

  主題句是表達一個中心思想的句子,因此不可以語意模糊不清。例如 "To dance well, you need to know something about dancing." 其中 "something about dancing" 語意模糊,若修改為 "To dance well, you need to have a good sense of rhythm." 就好多了。

- **主題句語意不可太廣泛 (not too broad)**

  語意太廣泛就無法將主題限制在一個段落裡,它可以是一篇文章的題目,但不是好的主題句。例如:"Computers have great influences on our daily lives." 這句話太廣泛,可修改為 "Computers make our life easier." 或者是更進一步的 "We can easily communicate with our friends who stay far away through e-mail."。

- **主題句必須是可討論的 (discussible)**

  例如 "Chinese New Year's Day falls on the first day on the lunar calendar." 只提出事實,缺乏討論的空間,不是適當的主題句。

主題句經常出現在第一句,一方面可以提醒作者段落發展的方向,另一方面也可以讓讀者抓住段落的中心思想。

Activity 2

以下 (1)～(4) 題中各有一組主題句，從其中選出比較不適當的一句，並說明原因。

_____ (1) a. My topic is my cat.

b. My pet, a black cat, is very curious.

_____

_____ (2) a. I have problems in senior high school.

b. My biggest problem is that I find it hard to concentrate in class.

_____

_____ (3) a. Arizona is a U.S. state located in the Southwestern United States.

b. Arizona is a very modern, urbanized state with a bit of industry and mechanized farming.

_____

_____ (4) a. Every student should learn how to get online to gather information.

b. Every student should learn something about computers.

_____

Activity 3

請指出每個段落的主題句並畫上底線。

(1) The kitten sends messages through its whiskers. When the whiskers are flat, they communicate fear. Pointing to the front, with ears pointing toward the rear, they show anger. On the other hand, the cat expresses happiness when its whiskers are relaxed.

(2) A well-trained kitten knows that it must not steal food. It has no right to climb on the dining table when the meal is prepared. It must eat from its own plate, and only what is prepared on it. This is not only good for its training but for its health as well.

(3) The Earth has warmed about 1 degree Fahrenheit in the last 100 years—more in some places, like the Arctic. Already we're seeing changes in Alaska, where roads are buckling in places and some major pipelines no longer fit together.

Coldwater fish that used to be found off the Alaska coast are no longer there, because the waters are too warm. Polar bears are having a terrible time there and may be extinct by the end of this century.

(4) It is difficult for a vast country to maintain one language as its official language. There are two main sources that help the English language to remain alive and in use in the United States. The first is the high rate of people moving within the country. This enables the language to travel, even to the most remote areas. The second is the high accessibility to different forms of oral media. Television and radios broadcast what can be called "standard American English" to a large population.

Activity 4

(1) 請由每一個段落下方的三個句子中，選出最適當的一句，作為段落的主題句。

A.

_____

They are everywhere—in big cities and small villages. They are living in places like abandoned buildings, temples, train stations and parks. The government can barely cope with the large number of homeless people. This is becoming a social problem worth paying more attention to.

a. Homeless people go from place to place because they want to live freely.

b. Today in Taiwan, homeless people are not easy to ignore.

c. The government pays more attention to homeless people.

B.

_____

Imagine buying a shirt only to discover that it doesn't fit. Or a lamp that looked much better in the picture than in your bedroom. Exchanging goods bought online can take several weeks, and customers may have to communicate with the Customer Service Department, rather than a salesperson. This lack of interpersonal communication can be difficult to get used to. After all, shopping has always been a social activity that includes bargaining and discussion.

a. The Internet has made shopping very convenient.

b. Online shopping has its drawbacks.

c. Lacking bargaining and discussion makes online shopping boring.

C.

For example, people in the U.S. eat a lot of meat and only a small amount of grains and vegetables. There is a high rate of cancer and heart disease. However, in Japan, people eat a large amount of grains and very little meat. There is a very low rate of cancer and heart disease. Besides, the Japanese live longer than any other people in the world. Doctors believe that too much animal fat can cause disease.

a. People in Japan have a healthy diet.

b. Too much animal fat is harmful to our health.

c. People everywhere in the world eat too much animal fat.

D.

Walking is really an ideal and natural form of physical exercise that people of all ages can routinely participate in. Whether you're strolling through a mall, hiking through a park, or walking your dog around the neighborhood, walking lifts your spirits, clears your mind, maintains or loses your weight, and increases your fitness. It also strengthens your bones and muscles, and reduces your risk of developing conditions such as heart disease or type 2 diabetes.

a. Walking is a great form of physical activity for people who are overweight.

b. Walking is an effective way of strengthening the mind and heart.

c. The easiest way to improve your health is to choose to walk at every possible opportunity.

(2) 請依據 2b 所述幾項原則，寫出以下四個段落的主題句。

A.

For example, anniversary cards are no longer just for "Mom and Dad." You can easily find anniversary cards for "Mom and her husband" and "Dad and his wife" because of the high rate of divorce and second marriages. You can also find cards for your friends who just lost their jobs, or lost a game. Maybe someday when you lose your weight, you'll receive a card for a person who "lost weight."

B.

We should get as much information as possible about the area we plan to go to. Our health must be in good condition. We must have the right clothing, the right equipment, and enough supplies, including some medicine. For possible emergencies, we should bring a compass, extra food and water. Careful planning is the key to a safe trekking in high mountains.

C.

The diaphragm is a muscle at the bottom of your lungs that helps you breathe. When the diaphragm is disturbed, the breath becomes a little irregular. As the irregular breath hits the voice box, which helps you speak, it becomes a sound, and that strange sound is a hiccup.

D.

For example, if you eat too fast or too much, or if you are very nervous or excited, you might get hiccups. Sometimes, breathing certain strong smells—such as perfume, gasoline or hair spray—can cause them. Or, eating a spicy food can sometimes make hiccups happen.

(3) 假設你要寫以下三篇作文，先做構思活動，然後寫出它們的主題句。

A. Rainy Days

B. Spring

C. The Most Terrible Trip

2c   支持句 *Supporting Sentences*

2c-1   概括性的與具體性的 *General and Specific*

主題句之後就要進入段落的第二個部分——支持句 (Supporting Sentences)。

主題句因為要表達段落的中心思想，語意上概括性較高 (general)，而支持句中的句子因為要詳細地闡述主題句，所以必須使用語意上比主題句明確的 (specific) 詞語。從 general 到 specific 是寫作時句子和句子之間很重要的邏輯次序之一。

 範例

(1) Bats perform an important ecological function throughout the world.
→ general
(2) They eat millions of harmful insects yearly. → specific
(3) In fact, the food a bat eats every night amounts to one quarter of its own body

weight. → more specific

說明 這三句之中,第一句是主題句,語意上概括性最高。第二、三句則較具體明確,用來闡述主題句。而第三句又比第二句明確,因為第三句更進一步的舉出細節來說明第二句。練習這樣的句子連貫在寫作時是很重要的。

　　何謂 "general" 和 "specific" 呢?以 music 和 jazz (爵士樂) 為例,music 涵蓋的範圍比較廣,是概括性較高的字,而 jazz 則比較明確,因為 jazz 只是 music 中的一部分。building material (建材) 和 brick (磚) 比較,building material 概括性比較高,brick 則比較明確。

　　在下面這兩個句子中,general 和 specific 的分別就非常清楚:

Stress has become a favorite **subject of everyday conversation**. It is not unusual to hear friends and family members talk about the difficulty they have in managing the stress of everyday life.

→第二句用 specific 的詞語來說明第一句很 general 的說法 (subject of everyday conversation)。

　　以下有四組句子,每一組的第一句用字比較籠統,而第二句比較明確。請詳細比較兩者之間的差異,看看比較明確的詞語是否讓描述更生動呢?

1. I love cakes. → general

   I love cheese cakes and chocolate cakes. → specific

   ✎ 第二句指出了哪類蛋糕。

2. My English teacher is a conservative dresser. → general

   My English teacher usually wears a gray suit and an old-fashioned necktie. → specific

   ✎ 第二句舉出了細節來描述穿著保守。

3. The group traveled through several countries on its concert tour last year. → general

   The group traveled through France, Germany and Canada on its concert tour last year. → specific

   ✎ 第二句明確地指出去了哪些國家。

4. A woman sat in front of the fire during the cold winter. → general

   An elderly woman wearing a faded red robe sat in front of the fire on a cold, rainy, and windy day. → specific

🖐第二句的 woman 前後用了形容詞和分詞片語描述，又用了 a cold、rainy 和 windy 等字使得這個句子的情境更具體明確。

Activity 1

下面每一題有三個句子，三個句子之間語意是連貫的。先找出概括性最高的句子，在前面標示 1，再找出比較明確和最明確的句子，分別標示 2 和 3。第一題為範例。

(1) ___2___ a. They eat millions of harmful insects yearly.

___3___ b. In fact, the food a bat eats every night amounts to one quarter of its own body weight.

___1___ c. Bats perform an important ecological function throughout the world.

(2) _____ a. The natural environment rarely escapes damage wherever large numbers of tourists are found.

_____ b. For example, the Sun Moon Lake has been polluted as a result of its tourist developments.

_____ c. The quality of water and air, and even the diversity of fish in the lake are affected in some way.

(3) _____ a. You don't have to read everything at the same speed.

_____ b. How fast you read often depends on your reason for reading.

_____ c. Reading is like riding a bicycle.

(4) _____ a. It extends from the Atlantic Ocean to the Pacific Ocean and shares land borders with Canada and Mexico.

_____ b. Its total area is over 3.7 million square miles, making it the fourth largest country in the world.

_____ c. The United States is a very large country.

(5) _____ a. Instead, polar bears remain active, hunting seals through the whole winter.

_____ b. Strictly speaking, polar bears do not hibernate.

_____ c. They do not experience a state of "deep hibernation."

(6) _____ a. Many historic sites have been saved from destruction because of tourists' interest in them.

_____ b. Conservation and tourism often go together hand in hand.

_____ c. Hundreds of historic houses in Paris might be only ruins if they held no value as tourist attraction.

(7) _____ a. Sometimes the natural environment has benefited from tourism.

_____ b. As a result, the parks and nature reserves have led to the protection of many species of wild animals.

_____ c. In order to attract tourists to East Africa, Kenya established huge national parks and game reserves.

(8) _____ a. Coaches represent a relatively cheap form of transportation to and around tourist destinations.

_____ b. Greece, for example, depends greatly on coach services for the movement of tourists.

_____ c. In countries where the construction of railroads is difficult, coaches are the main way of traveling around.

Activity 2

下面有六個概括性較高的句子，請針對它們寫出一至兩句有明確細節的句子。

(1) I got very nervous. _____

_____

(2) My mother loves to help people. _____

_____

(3) Judy has bad table manners. _____

_____

(4) My family members like to go out on weekends. _____

_____

(5) My mother encourages us to help out with household chores. _____

_____

(6) Edward is a moody person. _____

_____

2c-2 *How to Write Supporting Sentences* 支持句的寫法

　　支持句是段落的主體，想要把段落架構得穩固健全，就要讓支持句能和主題句有密切的關連，而且能充分地支持、闡明主題句，段落的發展才算完整。

1. 主題句寫好之後，段落要如何發展呢？要依循什麼方向呢？

　(1) 依照構思之後擬定的大綱寫成完整的段落。

　(2) 針對主題句 (尤其是主題論述) 提出問題。如果你看到題目，例如 **A Terrible Trip**，想出了主題句 "My trip in Nepal was extremely terrible."，就可以提出以下的問題來構思段落的方向和內容：

　　・ When did I go to Nepal?

　　・ Who did I go with?

　　・ What made the trip a terrible one?

　　・ How did I feel about what had happened?

> 好的支持句一定要能闡明主題句。在寫完段落之後，我們可以用 Who、What、How、When、Why、Where 之類的問題來檢視段落是否已充分發展。

2. 支持句的部分要如何組織來發展段落呢？

　　常用的技巧有：舉例 (examples)、細節 (details)、小故事 (anecdotes or stories)、事實或統計數字 (facts or statistics)、理由 (reasons)、解釋或說明 (explanations)、原因或結果 (cause/effect) 以及比較或對照 (compare/contrast)。這些方法可以單獨使用在一個段落中，也可以兩種以上合併使用。

(1) 舉例

主題句

　　Cats with their sixth sense appear to forecast disasters or the death of a loved one. For example, Sir Winston Churchill's cat leapt on his bed on the evening of January 25, 1965, and then left the room, meowing in a strange way. It sounded as if it were announcing the death of the great statesman, who died the next morning.

說明 舉邱吉爾的貓在他臨終前特別的舉動為例，說明貓有第六感。

(2) 細節

主題句

On Halloween night, a strange sight can be seen. Children wear strange costumes and spooky masks. They go from house to house in their neighborhood, knocking on every door they see. On hearing the knock, the neighbor will open the door. Then the children altogether shout, "Trick or treat, trick or treat!" After that, the neighbor will put some candy in the bag which child carries.

說明 支持句每一句都提出細節 (costumes, masks, knocking on the door, trick or treat, candy) 來說明 a strange sight。

(3) 小故事

主題句

Sometimes people are deceived by dress. Once a great scholar went to a party. As he was very simply dressed, he was not admitted into the party. So he returned home and put on his best suit. He went back to the party and was given a warm reception. In the course of dinner he did not eat but just talked to his clothes. The host came and asked what was the matter. The scholar told him what had happened. Since he was admitted for the sake of his fine dress, he would talk to his dress only. The host regretted it and apologized. Though dress may be, to some degree, useful to judge a person, that alone will not be enough.

(取自 81 年度日大試題)

說明 第二句之後是一則故事，它很具體地說明了主題句 "people are deceived by dress"。

(4) 統計數字

主題句

The Internet has replaced books as a major source of information for Taiwan primary school students. According to a recent survey conducted last December, 77 percent of the students considered the Internet to be the most convenient source of information. 14 percent of the respondents said they often turned to books for information instead of going online. Of all the students surveyed, only 27 percent had never used the Net.

(取自 92 年度指考考題)

說明 舉出調查結果 (一連串的百分比) 來證明 "the Internet has replaced books as a major source of information"。

(5) 解釋或理由

　　　　　　　　　　　　　　　　　　主題句
I like walking for three reasons. First, I can do it anytime and anywhere. An evening walk across the streets of a big city can be just as enjoyable as a morning stroll on a country road or a hike in the mountains. Second, I don't need any fancy equipment to take part in this activity. What I need is a good pair of shoes. Third, I can enjoy it with my friends or alone. When there happen to be friends around, I enjoy walking with them. Otherwise, walking alone is also a great joy to me.

說明 用了承轉語 First、Second 和 Third 來列舉出三項理由。

(6) 原因或結果

　　先列出某件事再說明它發生的原因，或者先提到某件事 (因) 再說明造成了什麼結果，另外也可以說明一連串互為因果的事。
　　　　　　　　　　　　　　　　　　　　主題句
　　As new materials develop, one invention often leads to another. Steel, for instance, was developed by engineers in the 19th century. Because of its strength, steel soon became a useful building material. With steel construction, buildings could then have a great many stories. But no one could be expected to walk up 8, 10, or 30 flights of stairs. Therefore, to make tall buildings more accessible to their users, the elevator was invented. By providing much-needed space in a world crowded with people, tall buildings have solved a great problem of the city and have completely changed our way of life.　　　　　　(取自 92 年度指考考題)

說明
・主題句 "one invention often leads to another" 就說明了因果關係。接下來舉 steel 為例來說明。
・ steel → buildings with a great many stories → elevator → tall buildings
・最後 tall buildings 林立的結果是解決都市擁擠的問題和改變了生活方式。

(7) 比較或對照

　　可以比較說明相同之處或對照說明相異之處。　　主題句
From a physiological standpoint, animals are completely different from plants. Animals are able to feel pain so that they can use it for self-protection. For example, if you touch something hot and feel pain, you will learn from this

discomfort that you should not touch that item in the future. On the other hand, plants cannot feel pain. This sensation is not necessary for them because they cannot move from place to place and do not need to learn to avoid certain things. Unlike animals' body parts, many fruits and vegetables can be harvested over and over again without dying.

說明 第一句是主題句，指出動物和植物在生理上是截然不同的。接下來的句子以先談動物再談植物的方式對照它們的不同。

Activity 3

以下有四個段落，細讀之後回答下面的問題。

(1)

　　Whenever a Dalai Lama died, a search began for his reincarnation. The chosen male child had to have certain qualities. One was the ability to identify the belongings of his predecessor, or rather his previous self. Another requirement was that he should have large ears, upward-slanting eyes and eyebrows. Besides, one of his hands should bear a mark like a conch-shell. 　　　(取自 93 年度學測考題)

A. 哪一句是主題句？

B. 支持句運用了什麼技巧？

C. 段落指出了幾項 qualities ？

(2)

　　Outbreaks of avian influenza can be devastating for the poultry industry and for farmers. For example, an outbreak of avian influenza in the USA in 1983–1984 resulted in the destruction of more than 17 million birds at the cost of nearly US$65 million. Economic consequences are often most serious in developing countries where poultry raising is an important source of income, and of food, for impoverished rural farmers and their families. When outbreaks become widespread within a country, control can be extremely difficult. Therefore, government authorities usually undertake aggressive emergency control measures as soon as an outbreak is detected. 　　　(取自 93 年度指考考題)

A. 支持句運用了什麼技巧？

B. 提出 17 million 和 US$65 million 這兩項數字有什麼目的？

C. 最後一句的目的是什麼？它和前一句之間是什麼關係？

(3)

Research about learning styles has identified gender differences. For example, one study found various differences between boys and girls in sensory learning styles. Girls were both more sensitive to sounds and more skillful at fine motor performance than boys. Boys, in contrast, showed an early visual superiority to girls. ⑤ They were, however, clumsier than girls. ⑥ They performed poorly at a detailed activity such as arranging a row of beads. But boys excelled at other activities that required total body coordination.　(取自 93 年度學測考題)

A. 哪一句是主題句？

B. 支持句運用了什麼技巧？

C. 第五句和第六句之間是什麼關係？

(4)

Red imported fire ants can cause a number of problems. They construct their colonies on precious farmland, invading crops while searching for insects underground. They also like to make their mounds in sunny areas, heavily infesting lawns and pastures. They can quickly strip fruit trees of their fruit. ⑤ They appear to be attracted to electromagnetic fields and attack electrical insulation or wire connections. ⑥ They can cause electrical shorts, fires, and other damage to electrical equipment. Worst of all, their stings can be fatal to livestock and humans.

(取自 94 年度學測考題)

A. 哪一句是主題句？

B. 支持句運用了什麼技巧？

C. 支持句總共指出了幾個方面紅火蟻造成的問題？分別是哪幾個方面？

D. 第五句和第六句之間是什麼關係？

Activity 4

請將以下每一題中一個或數個句子擴展為一個段落 (記得運用 specific 的概念和支持句的寫法)。

(1) Judy is the most hard-working student that I've ever seen.

(2) I like summer because during the season we students have a very long vacation.

(3) Don't worry about how you look. The most important thing you have to do is try to be an interesting person.

(4) Iris saw a kitten on her way from school. She held it in her arms and went home. It finally became her pet.

Concluding Sentences　結論句

　　結論句經常出現在正式段落文章的最後一句，它的功能是用來總結段落的文意，將讀者的注意力拉回主題句中。如果段落很短或主題清楚，支持句也能充分支持主題時，結論句是可以省略的。結論句的寫法大致有下列兩種：

1. 用不同的文字重述主題句、將段落文意做摘要或下結論。

　　A new type of virtual keyboard which appears on the computer screen can be used by the handicapped. You can either touch the key on the screen with your finger or a stylus, or use a mouse to indicate which key you want to press. This type of keyboard is very useful to some handicapped people, because you can put on a headset, and when you move your head, it acts like a mouse. You don't have to use your hands for anything. This on-screen virtual keyboard is designed with special consideration for the handicapped.

→此結論句是文意的摘要。

2. 預測未來或是提出呼籲、建議或解決方法等。

　　A little bit of stress can work in a positive way. For example, a stress reaction can sometimes save your life by releasing hormones that enable you to react quickly and with greater energy in a dangerous situation. In everyday situation, too, stress can provide that extra push needed to do something difficult. During a sports competition, stress might push you to perform better. Also, without the stress of deadlines, you might not be able to finish schoolwork or get to where you need to be on time. Stress is not always a kiss of death. Are you ready for a little positive stress?

→此結論句以問句的方式提出呼籲。

重述主題句和下結論最為常用，多練習這兩種寫法吧！

Activity

下有三個段落，請寫出適當的結論句。

(1)

Wellness means the best possible health within the limits of your body. One person may need fewer calories than another. Some people might prefer a lot of easier exercise to more challenging exercise. While one person enjoys playing seventy-two holes of golf a week, another would rather play three sweaty, competitive games of tennis. (取自 94 年度學測考題)

(2)

A positive attitude can motivate you to accomplish more in your life. Whenever something goes wrong, remember that you are the person who controls your reaction. Don't let others take that control away from you. If you start looking for things to go right, chances are that you will get the result you expect. Nothing can motivate you more than approaching each situation with a positive state of mind. A smile on your face and the right attitude can help you overcome even the most difficult problems.

(3)

Why have so many companies started allowing their employees to wear casual clothes? One reason is that it's easier for a company to attract new employees if it has a casual dress code. If the company has a conservative dress code, it's hard to hire people. Another reason is that people seem happier and more productive when they are wearing comfortable clothes. Most people believe that casual dress improves employee morale. Supporters of casual wear also argue that a casual dress code helps them save money because casual clothes are less expensive than suits. (取自 91 年度學測考題)

TEACHER'S NOTE

■英文作文中一定要有主題句嗎？它一定要在第一句嗎？

　　段落有一個表達中心思想的主題句是英文寫作的特色，它通常出現在第一句。雖然對專業的作家而言，這不是絕對必要的，但是對初學英文寫作的你，有主題句 (而且放在第一句) 是絕對有好處的。

好處 1：作文的第一句就開門見山，切入主題，使讀者或閱卷的老師能一目了然，知道這篇作文的中心思想是什麼。

好處 2：段落的支持句是根據主題句擴展的，而主題句在第一句，就像在監視你、提醒你勿偏離主題了。

■為什麼要學習 general 和 specific 的語詞？寫作文時真的用得上嗎？

　　主題句是段落中概括性最高的句子，而支持句是語意比較明確的句子，用來擴展主題句。因此你得學會用 specific 的語詞以明確表達句子的語意，更要會在一個 general 的句子之後寫出幾個 specific 的句子，這樣你寫的作文才會層次井然。

　　這方面的練習，對有些把作文寫得句句都像是主題句的同學是很有幫助的。以下一篇作文好比是一棵只有主幹的樹，而你要做的是添加一些枝葉和花朵，使它完整，也就是說你要運用 specific sentences 來描述細節，使段落主旨能夠充分發展。添加細節的文章請參閱第一章的 Teacher's Note。

> 　　The most precious thing in my room is my piano. My mother bought it for my birthday when I was four years old. It has been my companion for 13 years. When I am bored, I play the piano. When I am happy, I play it. When I am frustrated, I play the piano too, because it helps heal my sorrows. That's why it is the most precious thing in my room.

■平時要如何加強使用 specific words and sentences 的能力呢？

1. 閱讀時要去欣賞並且學習別人的用字遣詞和寫作技巧，別忘了你閱讀的就是別人的寫作成品。看到好的詞彙、句子，立刻熟記，自己寫作文時就可以模仿。
2. 多練習寫作，多做類似這一章所提供的 Activity。

 Have Fun!

Writing's Powerful Message

There was once a young man who, in his youth, professed a desire to become a "great" writer.

When asked to define "great," he said "I want to write stuff that the whole world will read, stuff that people will react to on a truly emotional level, stuff that will make them scream, cry, wail, howl in pain, desperation, and anger!"

He now works for Microsoft writing error messages.

Unity and Coherence
統一性及連貫性

▶ 要使段落完整而且流暢，除了上一章的寫作技巧之外，還要學習如何使段落有統一性及連貫性。

3a
統一性
Unity

　　統一性簡單的說就是一致性，每一段只談一個主題。段落中每一個句子都有同一個目的，就是支持主題句。任何一個句子都必須圍繞這個主題發展，不可以偏離主題。

3a-1　具有統一性的段落範例

　　What would happen if a big comet hit the Earth today? First, the comet would start to burn if it entered the Earth's atmosphere. Parts of the comet would either burn away or break off. The parts that remain would strike the planet at an incredible speed. The sea might heat up and start to boil. Huge waves would be created. Cities in many parts of the world would be destroyed.

說明 這個段落的主題是彗星如果撞地球會發生什麼事，而從第二句開始，每一句都在說明這些事，沒有一句偏離主題。

3a-2　學生常犯的錯誤

・下筆前沒有周詳的規劃，想到什麼就寫什麼。
・雖然寫了完整的主題句，卻在兩三個句子之後偏離了主題。
・雖然已經掌握了段落發展的方向，卻任意地在句與句中間加上一兩句與主題沒有關聯的句子。

LOOK

如何避免這些錯誤呢？方法一：寫作前先擬訂要點大綱。
方法二：時時回顧主題句中的 controlling idea。

Activity 1

請指出以下兩個段落，哪一個具有一致性？哪一個缺少一致性？

(1)

For millions of fans, Christopher Reeve will always be Superman. He was taking part in a jumping competition in May 1995, when he was thrown off his horse. But he died of heart failure at 52 in 2004. This serious accident changed his life overnight. After the accident, he tried hard to live an active life. He established a foundation, battling for finding treatments and cures for spinal cord injuries. Reeve first gained renown when he was selected from 200 candidates to play the title character in the 1978 movie *Superman*. Hollywood was kind to him after the accident. Offers came in for directing, acting and voice work.

(2)

When the first Superman movie was released, Reeve was frequently asked, "What is a hero?" He would say that a hero is someone who commits a brave act without thinking of the consequences. After that accident, his answer changed. He believed that a hero is an ordinary person with the strength to continue despite obstacles. Christopher Reeve was truly a hero—first as Superman and later as himself.

Activity 2

以下有四個段落，每一段中都有一句或不只一句不切合主題的句子，請找出並畫上底線。

(1)

Watching TV is the only way my son spends his leisure time. He is so interested in almost every program on TV that TV becomes his faithful companion. He is a college student. He feels comfortable whenever he gets any chance to lie on the couch, watching sports, the Discovery Channel, or any films. With a remote control in his hand, he can even switch channels without getting up. This is the only thing he loves to do in his free time.

(2)

Swimming is a good form of exercise. It can strengthen our hearts and our lungs. It also helps circulation. Like other sports, it helps to develop strong muscles. Many schools offer children athletic programs. Even the disabled can swim to keep their bodies in better condition. So, doctors suggest that we learn to swim at an early age.

(3)

People in Scotland celebrate New Year in a special way. On New Year's Eve when the last minute comes, a song called "Auld Lang Syne" is sung. Almost all the people in English-speaking countries know the song. I like the song very much. It tells people to remember the past and look forward to the future. People also believe that the first person to enter their home after midnight can bring them good luck. So if someday you are the first person to visit them after midnight, be sure to carry bread and money so that the family will not be hungry or poor in the coming year.

(4)

Flash mobs have become popular around the world. Most flash mobs last less than ten minutes, and many are completed in less than one minute. Some experts say that's because they give people a chance for some excitement in their daily lives. Others call flash mobs a new kind of performance art. A few experts have even suggested that people like flash mobs because they are social activities where people can meet other people. And most participants agree that they provide people with comic relief in the busy and stressful modern world.

3b 連貫性 Coherence

連貫性指的是：

(1) 段落中所有的句子都按照一定的邏輯次序組合起來，句子與句子之間的邏輯關係清楚，使內容成為有意義的整體，讓讀的人能完全瞭解內容要表達的意義。

(2) 句子和句子之間的語氣要順暢。

邏輯不清，語無倫次經常是學生寫作時最麻煩的問題，以下為邏輯關係不清楚的句子：

A. I enjoy my job very much. Many people ask me questions. I give them the necessary information.

　→什麼工作會碰到很多人？為什麼喜歡這份工作？

B. I had a toothache last Wednesday. I was terrified of dentists. The next day the dentist made an examination and found a cavity.

　→當天去看牙醫了沒？為什麼怕牙醫？檢查後有治療嗎？

這些句子沒有把話說清楚，句子和句子之間少了一些說明，邏輯就不夠清楚，讀的人會覺得不知所云，起了很多疑問。

仔細看看補了哪些文字可以讓疑問得到了解答，也使這些句子有了連貫性：

A. As an information desk clerk, I meet all kinds of people while I am doing my job. Many people ask me questions, and I give them the necessary information they need. I always try to be very helpful. I enjoy my job because I find joy in helping others.

B. I had a toothache last Wednesday. I hesitated to go to the dentist because I was terrified of dentists. When I finally went there, it was the next day. The dentist made a check and told me that the pain was caused by a cavity. Once again, I had another horrible experience of having my tooth drilled.

解決方法

- 加一些句子讓邏輯清楚、內容完整易懂。
- 加上 while、and、because、finally、but、once again、another 等承轉語 (transitions) 讓文字語氣順暢。

3b-1　達到連貫性的方法一：邏輯次序

　　段落組成有一定的章法與邏輯次序，這個次序本身就是一種表達連貫的方式。不同性質的段落，它的內容就有不同的安排次序：

> 要使段落合乎邏輯次序，在擬訂大綱時就要先排出這些順序。

(1) 敘述事件和說明過程按照時間順序。

範例

　　Early one morning, my dog Milo began to behave strangely. While I was dressing for work, Milo stood at the window of my apartment, watching the street below. He barked excitedly; meanwhile, I got my bag and left the apartment. I walked down the stairs and **then** opened the door onto the street. While **a moment later**, Milo jumped out of the window above me! He landed with a crash, then immediately got up and started running. **Soon after**, I saw what he was excited about: another dog playing with a ball. I watched as Milo quickly grabbed the dog's ball, and ran away. I followed Milo, and eventually found him in the park, playing with the ball as if nothing had happened. **At last**, I took him home and finally arrived at work—more than two hours late!

說明

・這個段落敘述一個小事件的過程，按照時間順序安排要點。

・此處使用表示時間順序的承轉語 (粗體字部分)。

(2) 按照空間順序描述人、物、地方、海報或繪畫等，次序可以是由近到遠或由遠到近、由裡到外或由外到裡、由上到下或由下到上，或先描述主體再描述次要的部分。

範例

　　My office is at the very top of our house. To visit me, first climb the twenty steep stairs leading from the street and open the front door. Walk **along the corridor ahead**; on both sides, you'll see lots of framed family photos. **At the**

end of the corridor is a living room and **in the corner** are thirty more steep stairs leading up to my office. Climb **up** the stairs and straight in front you'll see my desk with a computer. **To the right** of the desk, there are big windows looking out to the sea. **On the opposite** wall, there are shelves filled with books. **Next to** the shelves is a red door leading out to a roof garden. **In the center of** the garden, there are comfortable chairs to relax in—perfect after climbing all those stairs!

說明
- 這是一篇按照空間順序安排要點的段落。
- 以由下往上的順序引導讀者：street → living room → office → roof garden。
- 在第 2～4 句中，還有由近到遠的順序：the front door → along the corridor ahead → at the end...。
- 描述空間位置時用了表空間的承轉語 (粗體字部分)。

(3) 說明理由、結果、或提出細節來解釋事物的順序可以是：從簡單到複雜、從比較重要到最重要、從比較不明顯到最明顯、從不熟悉到熟悉、從概括性高 (general) 到具體明確 (specific) 等。

範例

　　Harry Potter has captured the world's attention for many reasons. **First**, the *Harry Potter* books are easy to read, so they appeal both to children and to adults. **What's more**, Harry Potter lives in an exciting, colorful fantasy world, which we all love to explore as if we were really there, through reading about his adventures. **Next**, the *Harry Potter* books have a whole host of loveable characters— including Hermione Granger, Ron Weasley and Uncle Vernon—who readers can't help wanting to know more about. **More importantly**, the *Harry Potter* books, which tell wonderful stories of danger, mystery and adventure, are hard to put down once you've started reading. And, **last but not least**, there's Harry himself. He's funny, clever and interesting, and everyone wants to find out about his life, as he goes from one amazing situation to another, throughout the series of stories.

說明
- 這個段落按照重要性的順序來說明 *Harry Potter* 讓全世界都注意它的理由。
- 每一項要點之前都有表次序的承轉語 (粗體字部分)。

(4) 討論因果關係的次序可以先敘述觀察到的現象(因)，再談它造成的問題 (果)，
最後提出解決之道 (這個部分不一定要提供)。

範例

　　Mental illness, including severe depression and psychosis, is a significant problem in the United States. An estimated one of five Americans will suffer from some type of mental illness in the course of a year. **One tragic effect** of untreated mental illness is that many of these people become **homeless**. They have no job and no income, which forces them to live on the streets and beg for food. Sadly, many of these people were once productive members of society, with jobs, families and homes. However, when faced with untreated mental illness, these people often lose their jobs and homes. Public officials are taking action to help solve social problems relating to mental illness, including **making laws** that force insurance companies to pay for treatment, and **beginning new programs** for homeless people that get them off the streets and into safe, caring environments, such as treatment centers and homeless shelters.

說明

· 這個段落先敘述觀察到的現象 mental illness，再談它造成 homeless 的問題，
　最後提出解決之道：making laws...beginning new programs....。
· 此段落的邏輯關係為：因造成果，這個果也是另一個因，造成了另一個果。

Activity 1

　　仔細讀完段落，回答之後的問題。

(1)

　　The types of tea are distinguished by their processing. Black tea preparation consists mainly of picking young leaves and leaf buds on a clear sunny day and letting the leaves dry for about an hour in the sun. Then, they are lightly rolled and left in a fermentation room to develop scent and a red color. Next, they are heated several more times. Finally, the leaves are dried in a basket over a charcoal fire.

(取自 95 年度學測考題)

A. 段落的要點是按照哪種邏輯次序安排的？
B. 段落中用了哪幾個承轉語？

(2)

[1] E-mail is instant, traveling from point to point. [2] With it, geography is no obstacle and time is not important. [3] I can zap a message to Kenya whenever I want to, and it gets there almost in a second. [4] The ease of this kind of writing and sending probably makes for a different kind of communication. [5] I can complain about the breakfast I had this morning or rattle on about friends and movies. [6] That is because I am not so focused on style and profundity. [7] I might be less likely to say something deeper. [8] My brother might glance at my mail, have a laugh, and then delete it. (取自 95 年度指考考題)

A. 前三句之間是什麼邏輯關係？

B. 第五和第六句之間是什麼邏輯關係？

C. 第七和第八句之間是什麼邏輯關係？

Activity 2

每一個段落之後有兩個或三個句子，依適當的順序填入空格裡使文意連貫。

(1)

When you are making preparation for your speech, do not try to memorize it word by word. This can turn out to be disastrous. ＿＿＿＿＿＿ ＿＿＿＿＿＿ You can rely on keywords to prompt your thoughts. But you need to know the structure of your speech and the information it contains very well.

A. Remember the outline of your presentation instead.

B. If you forget a single word, you might then forget everything that follows.

(2)

When giving an oral presentation, make sure you do not speak too fast. ＿＿＿＿＿＿ ＿＿＿＿＿＿ Try to channel your nervous energy by walking confidently, if your legs are rubbery, or by gesturing vigorously if your hands are shaking.

A. Pausing at appropriate times will not only allow you to catch your breath, but also control the audience's attention.

B. You should try to convey confidence to the audience, no matter how nervous you are.

(3)

Starbucks began in 1971 with a single-location coffee wholesale outlet in Seattle's Pike Place Market. _____ _____ _____ It will be interesting to see if the rest of the world is as easily influenced by trendy marketing plans, or if Starbucks might have to try a little harder to earn customer loyalty abroad.

A. Its global expansion has been very successful.

B. It is opening thousands of stores from Asia to South America, and to Europe.

C. Now it becomes the fastest-growing chain in the world.

(4)

Yesterday Mrs. Smith saw Judy, her neighbor's daughter, playing with her ball outside a drugstore. _____ _____ _____ But Mrs. Smith didn't run after her or told the owner about it. What she did was stare in amazement.   (取自 83 年度聯考考題)

A. Judy then ran off down the street.

B. Suddenly, Judy stopped playing and glanced around to see if anyone was looking.

C. The next moment, Mrs. Smith saw Judy put out her hand and take a peach from one of the boxes nearby.

(5)

Critics have called for changes to the education system. _____ _____ _____ But it is also important for students to be able to understand the reasons behind these numbers.

A. For example, they say it is not enough for students to learn that the Great Wall is 10,500 kilometers long.

B. Of course, it is important to know dates, facts, and figures.

C. Students should also learn why it was built, what effects it had on the world, and how it affects students in Taiwan today.

3b-2 達到連貫性的方法二：承轉語

在 3b 的修正句子中，加了 while、and、because、finally、but、once again 等字詞讓文字語氣順暢。這些用字都是承轉語，用來使句子之間的關係更清楚，有時也用來預告語氣或話題的轉換。

範例 I

These changes challenged many of the traditional roles men and women were expected to play. As a result, it is not uncommon nowadays to find women working outside their homes and being very concerned about their careers and personal lives.　　　　　　　　　　　　　　　　(取自 95 年度指考考題)

說明 as a result 可以使上下兩句的因果關係更清楚。

範例 II

At first glance, *Ally McBeal* appeared to be a show about lawyers. But when viewers looked deeper, they discovered it was really a show about women and relationships.

說明 but 預告語氣要轉換了。

範例 III

Fans of professional baseball and football argue continually over which is America's favorite sport. Though the figures on attendance for each vary with every new season, certain arguments remain the same. To begin with, football is a quicker, more physical sport, and football fans enjoy the emotional involvement they feel while watching. Baseball, on the other hand, seems more mental, like chess, and attracts those fans that prefer a quieter, more complicated game. In addition, professional football teams usually play no more than fourteen games a year. Baseball teams, however, play almost every day for six months. Finally, football fans seem to love the half-time activities, the marching bands, and the pretty cheerleaders. On the contrary, baseball fans are more content to concentrate on the game's finer details and spend the breaks between innings filling out their own private scorecards.　　(取自 95 年度學測考題)

說明
- 以 to begin with、in addition 和 finally 來分成三項說明。
- on the other hand 表達前後兩句的對比關係；however 則是預告話題轉換，要談 baseball；而 on the contrary 則表達前後兩句的對比關係。

以下為常用的承轉語列表：

Time	after before at first shortly when while later on in the meantime afterwards at that moment at last soon after by the time from then on
Space	above below farther on to the right/left nearby in front/back of opposite to far away from at the center on the outside
Sequence	first..., second..., third... in the first place next finally last but not least one...the other/another... to conclude with
Addition	and in addition besides moreover also furthermore too what's more to put it another way
Example	for example for instance such as including for one thing..., for another...
Cause/Effect	because for therefore so thus consequently accordingly as a result so...that...
Conclusion	in conclusion to summarize in summary to sum up in a word in short/brief on the whole all in all
Compare/ Contrast	likewise similarly in the same way but while however in contrast on the contrary on the other hand instead

承轉語就像是路標，能使文章連貫流暢並指引讀者你的文思或語氣要轉變了。因此學習使用承轉語是很重要的。

Activity 3

　　以下有三個段落，請依上下文意從下列的承轉語中選出適當者填入空格中，使段落語氣流暢。(需視情況做大小寫的變化，並且不可重複)

in fact	but	for instance	in addition	also	first
for example	in contrast	because	therefore	then	

(1)

　　On 3 October 2003, Participacíon Ciudadana, a citizens' group in Ecuador started a government-backed national movement against lateness. Offices, schools, and other institutions put up posters promoting punctuality, and people were not allowed to enter meetings late, to encourage respect for time. (A)_____, Switzerland will never need to fight lateness in this way, as the Swiss are famous for their punctuality. (B)_____, their postal system guarantees the nationwide delivery of letters within one working day, and approximately 98% of all mail reaches precisely on time. (C)_____, although e-mail has replaced letters to some extent, the postal department's profit was $302 million from January to June 2004—three times the profit from the same period in 2003.

(2)

　　There are mental methods to make our memory stronger. Repeating things—like grocery lists and appointments—aloud will make us remember them more. Recalling numbers is (A)_____ a mental exercise. This is how it works: (B)_____ write down a 10-digit number and (C)_____ try memorizing the digits one at a time. Use this technique often by trying to memorize phone, credit card and personal identification numbers. Another effective brain workout is to concentrate on our surroundings. (D)_____, we can sit down in our kitchen and try to recall and write down the contents of our bedroom. Focusing on one thing for a time can benefit our memory.

(3)

　　Most people like to talk, (A)_____ few people like to listen. Yet listening well is a rare talent that everyone should treasure. (B)_____ they hear more, good listeners tend to know more and to be more sensitive to what is going on around them than other people. (C)_____ , good listeners are inclined to accept or tolerate rather than judge and criticize. Therefore, they have fewer enemies than other people. (D)_____, they are probably the most loved of people.

(取自 88 年度推甄考題)

Activity 4

　　以下每一個段落都缺了一個包含有承轉語的句子，請選擇這個句子應該要放在 A、B 或 C 裡面。

(1)

　　Boldt Castle was named after its builder George Charles Boldt.　(A)　It started to be constructed in 1897 and was intended to be built as the Boldt's summer home and a present for George's wife, Louise.　(B)　Upon completion, it was to be spectacular.　(C)　She died of pneumonia at the age of 42.

・ _____　However, in January of 1904, all work upon the castle was stopped when Mrs. Boldt died.

(2)

　　The word aerobic means "with oxygen." Aerobic exercise refers to physical workouts that require oxygen to be delivered to the muscles over an extended period.　(A)　Aerobic activities such as jogging and swimming are typically sustained for a period of time, rather than short bursts of effort.　(B)　Anaerobic exercise refers to fitness routines that don't rely on oxygen for fuel.　(C)　Anaerobic workouts typically involve short burst of energy, which are powered by non-oxygen fuel sources stored in the muscles.

・ _____　On the other hand, the word anaerobic means "without oxygen."

(3)

　　It was not until 1901 that a person went over Niagara Falls in a barrel. Over the years 16 people have gone over the falls in a barrel and 6 of them died in the attempt.　(A)　The last person to try was Canadian Dave Murphy in 1993.　(B)　Their excuse was that it was too dangerous for the daredevils.　(C)　Another reason was that the stunts could cause damage to the falls because the rocks are very soft and easily broken. The stunts are now illegal and can result in a fine of US$10,000.

・ _____　After that, both the Canadian and American governments banned people from going over the falls.

(4)

　　In earthquake prone areas like Taiwan, Japan, and California, the premiums (what the insurance company charges for insurance coverage) are very high. ___(A)___ That is because earthquakes are completely unpredictable and can cause widespread damage. The insurers can't estimate when, or where an earthquake may occur. ___(B)___ They also can't estimate how much damage an earthquake may cause. In other words, they can't assess the risk of loss. ___(C)___

・ _____ For these reasons, most of the big insurance companies refuse to sell earthquake insurance.

(5)

　　The Thousands Island Region extends about 60 miles in length, from Lake Ontario up to the cities of Ogdensburg, NY. The total number of islands in this region is about 1,800. ___(A)___ The Treaty of Ghent, which formally ended the War of 1812, established the boundary line between Canada and the US. ___(B)___ They decided that no island shall be divided by the boundary line. They did attempt to divide the land acreage equally between the two countries. ___(C)___

・ _____ In the end, the result is that 2/3 of the islands are Canadian and 1/3 are US.

(6)

　　The Segway is currently being used by the Chicago Police Department to patrol O'Hare International Airport. ___(A)___ With miles of area to patrol and 200,000 travelers a day to serve and protect, the Segway has proven useful. ___(B)___ Because the Segway can travel up to 20 kilometers per hour, security officers can cover more area in less time than they could by just walking. ___(C)___

・ _____ For example, an officer can cover 8 to 10 miles of territory in less than half the time it took to patrol on foot.

3b-3 達到連貫性的方法三：重複關鍵字

　　在寫文章時，可以利用代名詞、同義詞或平行的結構來重複關鍵字，以使句與句之間具有連貫性。請閱讀以下的段落，並注意畫底線的部分：

The government has launched a scheme that children can eat breakfast at school. The scheme is especially aimed at children from low-income families.

說明 重複關鍵字 scheme。

The first book to be printed in movable type in English was about the history of Troy. It was printed in Flanders in 1474 by an Englishman, William Caxton. In 1476 he returned to England and established a printing press at Westminster.

說明 使用代名詞 It 和 he。

Many entertainment celebrities attended an anti-piracy demonstration in Taipei. The purpose of the rally was to ask fans to respect the copyright and to stop buying pirated CDs.

說明 使用了與 demonstration 意思相近的字 rally。

There is nothing magical about organic gardening. It is simply a way of working with nature rather than against it, of recycling natural materials to maintain soil fertility rather than relying on chemicals.

說明 在同一個句子中使用相同的文法結構 「...of V-ing...rather than..., of V-ing...rather than...」，使得結合更緊密。

Most of us have learned to vary our language and our behavior to meet the needs of different circumstances. We may feel free to yell and shout at children when we are angry with them, but we are usually very careful about raising our voices to our bosses or to someone superior. We may tease our friends or joke around with them, yet we tend to be more serious with strangers. Likewise, we may accept hugs and kisses from other members of our family, but many of us get uneasy when people we don't know very well touch us. (取自 83 年大學入學考試)

說明 同樣用 "We may..., but/yet...." 的結構，除了達成這三個句子的連貫，也讓主旨表達得更強而有力。

Activity 5

以下標示 1 和 2 的句子是兩個段落的主題句，而 A 到 F 共有六個句子是這兩個段落的支持句。由這六個選項中各選出三個句子並依照邏輯次序連貫成段落 (將字母代號填入空格內)。

(1) Tattoos have been around for thousands of years.

_____   _____   _____

(2) Although tattoos are popular today, they have not always been so.

_____   _____   _____

A. Later, tattoos became popular in Greece, the Middle East, and China.

B. Tattooing was also considered to be dangerous due to its unsanitary conditions.

C. A lot of people believed that only criminals had tattoos.

D. They then also spread to islands in the Pacific Ocean.

E. In the past, tattoos received bad reputation.

F. The earliest tattoos were probably created in Egypt.

Exercises

I. 以下每一題都有個主題句，將其下的句子按正確順序重組成有連貫性的段落，並填入主題句後面。

1. Baseball is one of America's most popular sports. ___ ___ ___ ___

   A. A player who goes around all the bases scores a run for his team.

   B. The team that finishes with more runs wins the game.

   C. In a baseball game there are two teams of nine players.

   D. Players must hit a ball with a bat and then try to run around four bases.

2. Credit cards are common these days. ___ ___ ___ ___

   A. Consumers consider credit cards to be very useful and convenient.

   B. As a result, they don't have to carry a large sum of money with them.

   C. They can use their cards in many shops and restaurants.

   D. And if they find themselves unexpectedly in need of money, they can use their credit cards to get cash from certain banks.

3. Recent scientific studies have shown that tears actually have a purpose: to keep you healthy. ___ ___ ___ ___

   A. If these chemicals are not released, then they will stay in your body and may make you sick.

   B. You are more likely to get a cold or develop a stomachache if you hold back your tears.

   C. According to scientists, when you are upset or in an emotional situation, harmful chemicals build up in your body.

   D. To get rid of these chemicals, your body uses tears to wash out these harmful substances.

4. The city of Seattle, in Washington State, is using Segways. ___ ___ ___ ___

   A. It costs only about US$0.01 a mile to run a Segway.

   B. The city is impressed with the low maintenance and operating costs of the Segway.

C. The city also likes Segways because they make no noise and there are no harmful exhaust emissions that pollute the air.

D. They are being used in trials to transport utility meter-readers from house to house to read water and electric meters.

II. 下面每一個段落都有不連貫之處，運用學過的方法作適當的修正。

1.

Tattoos had several purposes. Getting a tattoo was for decoration. Tattoos were used to identify different tribes or groups. Tattoos were used to show that a child had become an adult. Sailors liked to get tattoos as souvenirs of the places they had visited.

2.

Social attitudes about tattoos have changed. People with tattoos are no longer seen as criminals or troublemakers. Tattoos have become very common among movie stars and pop singers. It is hard to think of a famous person without one. More and more average people are getting tattoos. They are mothers and even grandmothers.

3.

A healthy breakfast gives children an advantage in life. Scientific studies have proved that children who eat a healthy breakfast concentrate better at school. Children are less likely to misbehave or miss classes. Children that eat breakfast generally do not overeat in the day. They are less likely to develop obesity.

4.

Helen Keller was born a healthy baby in 1880. At 18 months, Helen suffered an illness that caused Helen to lose her sight and her hearing. Helen was raised almost like a caged beast with no discipline or education. No one could communicate with her. When Helen was six, her parents hired Annie Sullivan, a twenty-year-old teacher who had been blind herself, to teach Helen.

■如何才能避免犯統一性方面的錯誤呢？

1. 完成構思之後，在擬訂大綱時，就要選擇和主題有密切關係的要點。之後，謹記要依循大綱來寫，才不至於思緒繁雜而偏離主題。有些同學想到有趣的要點，明知與主題無關但就是捨不得刪掉，想秀一下，結果成了作文中的毒瘤。
2. 寫完之後，用大綱來幫你檢視一下文章是否具有統一性。

■如何才能避免犯連貫性方面的錯誤呢？

其實連貫性可以分為意義的連貫性和文字語氣的連貫性。「意義的連貫性」就是文意或思緒要有邏輯次序。「文字語氣的連貫性」就是使用關鍵詞、代名詞以及承轉語，使段與段和句與句之間的語氣順暢。所以這個問題要分兩方面來回答。

1. 避免犯意義連貫性錯誤的方法：

  (1) 下筆之前要根據這章所學的原則，規劃好你的要點次序。

    假設你要介紹臺灣人的迷信，你一會兒寫醫院沒有四樓，因為四聽起來像死，不吉利。一會兒寫送禮不可以送鐘，「送終」當然不吉利。又寫數字六和八會帶來好運、過年時不能掃地…等等。這就是沒有次序。你應該分成數字、送禮、春節等不同的類別來寫。假設你要介紹好朋友，就分成外表、個性、彼此的互動及情感來談，由外而內，由具體進而抽象。這就是邏輯次序。

  (2) 選擇正確的字詞來使用，文法要正確。

    批改作文時，經常發現同學因為用字不當或文法錯誤，造成前後句子思緒不連貫或邏輯不通。例如：

    While other parents complain about their children's fooling around or not studying hard, my parents take a different attitude toward my academic performance. They are not like me to sit at my desk all day. They often say, "You don't have to study so hard to get the best grades."

    這是誤用 like 的例子，應該是 do not like me to V (不喜歡我去做某事) 而非 are not like me (不像我)。

2. 避免犯文字語氣連貫性錯誤的方法：

(1) 熟悉承轉語的運用

有些文體甚至有特定承轉語，這些在書中都有介紹，一定要好好學習。

(2) 小心使用代名詞

同學在使用代名詞時非常容易犯的錯誤，就是任意轉換人稱，沒有一致性。所以你在寫完作文之後一定要檢查是否有這類的錯誤。下面就有幾個句子讓你來檢查：

> Computers are playing an important role in our daily life. In companies, they need computers to help us deal with many complicated tasks. In laboratories, researchers need computers to help do their research. At home, housewives use computers to make our houses tidy and clean. You cannot do without computers in your life.

改正後的句子如下：

> Computers are playing an important role in our daily life. In companies, people need computers to help them deal with many complicated tasks. In laboratories, researchers need computers to help do their research. At home, housewives use computers to make their houses tidy and clean. We cannot do without computers in our life.

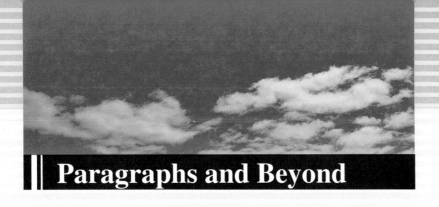

Paragraphs and Beyond

Paragraph Writing Practice
段落寫作練習

▶一篇字數 120 字左右的作文，是可以在一個段落中完成的，因此本章以段落寫作為目標。以下有九個單元，每個單元有五個左右的題目可以練習寫作。

L👀K

寫作前的步驟一：構思、寫要點大綱，步驟二：寫主題句，步驟三：寫支持句，步驟四：寫結論句。另外還要注意兩點原則，一：要點的安排要合乎邏輯次序，二：段落要有統一性和連貫性。

4a

敘述故事
Telling a Story

4a-1　敘述故事時需注意的要點

· 通常都用過去式。

· 須交代清楚 who、where、when、what、how、why 這些要素。

美國作家 James Thurber 寫了一本非常有趣的 *Fables for Our Time*《現代寓言集》。幾乎每一個寓言故事一開始就會交代出 when、who、where、what 等要素。例如在 "The Unicorn in the Garden" 這篇故事裡的第一句——Once upon a sunny morning a man who sat in a breakfast nook looked up from his scrambled eggs to see a white unicorn....。或是在 "The Sheep in Wolf's Clothing" 裡的第一句——Not very long ago there

Fables for Our Time
James Thurber
(1894~1961)

were two sheep who put on wolf's clothing and went among the wolves as spies, to see what was going on. 。

· 將細節按時間順序安排。

· 多使用承轉語 (表時間順序的承轉語列在 3b-2)。

4a-2 範例

題目

　　網路 (the Internet) 讓我們生活方便，但是也帶來了困擾。請敘述一則小故事來強調某個困擾。這故事可以是報章雜誌報導過的事件、你自己或身邊的朋友發生過的事情。

提示

· 說故事不一定要有主題句。而結論句的部分可以採用下結論、提出警示或呼籲的方式。

· 最好故事一開始就交代發生的事情、時間、地點等。

參考範文

Ｉn October 2002, police came to the hospital where Dr. Paul Grout worked and arrested him for buying cocaine online.

[ko`ken] *n.* [U] 古柯鹼

Paul denied the charges, but the police didn't believe him. After the arrest, the police went to Paul's house and searched his house and computers. They found no cocaine. Even so, Paul went to trial for buying illegal cocaine because the police said his credit card records proved he had bought it. Luckily, the doctor was able to prove—based on his work records—that he couldn't have possibly purchased it on the Internet. He was not even near computers at the times when some of the cocaine was purchased. The police eventually discovered that someone had stolen Paul's "identity" and was using his credit card numbers to commit crimes. This terrible story shows the dangers of identity theft and how it can ruin your life.

Activity

1. 下面的漫畫中，第二張圖不見了。猜一猜發生了什麼事。然後把第一張到第四張發生的事寫成一個故事。

2. 請完成以下的故事。

　　I once lived in Taipei, and worked as a volunteer in a hospital. It really felt good to get the opportunities to help people. One morning an elderly woman....

提示 說故事時，一開始就要交代場景。現在時間、地點、人物都出現了，接下來要寫的是發生了什麼事，結局又是如何呢？

3. 以大約 120～150 字寫出你最喜歡的一部電影中的情節。

4. 哪一則童年讀過的故事或寓言讓你印象深刻？以 120～150 字敘述故事的內容。

5. 你一定做過夢，不管是恐怖的、荒謬的還是喜悅的。以 **A Dream I Have Had** 敘述夢裡發生的事。

敘述故事，例如電影情節，不需要把所有發生的細節都寫出來。
也就是要會取捨，捨去細微末節，抓住主軸即可。

4b-1 描述經驗或事件時需注意的要點

· 和敘述故事一樣要交代在何時何地發生了什麼事，但更著重在描寫你的感覺，要讓讀者覺得身歷其境。
· 和敘述故事時相同，要注意時間順序。

4b-2 範例

題目

　　在你生活中曾經有過讓你恐懼、尷尬、不愉快或難以忘懷的經驗嗎？任選以下的題目寫出這個經驗：

(1) A Frightening Experience　　(3) A Good Memory That Will Last Forever
(2) The Most Embarrassing Moment　(4) A Day I'll Never Forget

提示

· 敘述這些經驗時，可以多描述一些細節和運用形容詞或比喻來描寫你的感受。
· 不一定要有主題句，但是在文字上要抓住讀者興趣，讓他們能一起分享你的經驗。

參考範文

　　As an American residing in Japan for five years, I had many embarrassing moments. Among them, the worst happened at a noisy bistro one evening. My friend and I had exited the elevator into the crowded restaurant lobby to wait for a table. While waiting, I noticed the elevator doors didn't close completely and I wondered if they could close with my hand between them. So, the next time the doors slid closed, I put out my hand, and it got stuck. It wasn't painful. However, since the elevator departed, the doors wouldn't open. Just then, our table was ready. I couldn't move and had to explain this predicament to my companion. This was extremely humiliating, as others waiting noticed my stuck hand and became concerned. Thankfully, the doors popped open again, as the elevator returned with more diners. Being in such an uncomfortable situation taught me to be more careful.

Vocabulary

- predicament [ˌprɪˈdɪkəmənt] *n.* [C] 窘境
- humiliating [hjuˈmɪlɪˌetɪŋ] *adj.* 丟臉的

Activity

1. 諺語是前人智慧的結晶。請從下列四個諺語中任選一個，並且以一件你本人發生的事情來說明。這件事必定讓你有所醒悟，瞭解了這個道理。

   (1) Laugh, and the whole world laughs with you. Weep, and you weep alone.

   (2) A friend in need is a friend indeed.

   (3) Practice makes perfect.

   (4) There is no place like home.

2. 你和家人一起去旅行過嗎？你參加過班遊嗎？你對畢業旅行的感覺如何？請選擇下列的題目，寫下這次旅遊的過程和你的感覺。

   (1) A Trip to Remember   (2) A Terrible Trip

   (3) The Most Unforgettable Trip I've Ever Had

3. 你有過打工的經驗嗎？有幫助陌生人的經驗嗎？有贏了或輸了比賽的經驗嗎？請以 **My Experience in...** 為題，寫下當時的情形。

4. 你記得第一次上臺講話的時候嗎？很緊張還是很興奮呢？請以 **The First Time I Spoke to the Whole Class** 為題，寫下這個經驗。

說明程序
Explaining a Process

4c-1   說明程序時需注意的要點

・要在一開始清楚地點明你的目的。
・要點的安排必須符合邏輯。
・多使用承轉語 (表次序的承轉語列在 3b-2)。

> **LOOK**
>
> 在說明過程時請隨時注意你所「述說的對象」是誰，
> 藉以調整文章的用字、語氣與內容。

4c-2   範例

題目

　　你有替同學或家人籌劃慶生會的經驗嗎？請以 **How to Plan a Birthday Party** 或 **How to Plan a Surprise Party** 為題寫出過程。

提示

・每一個步驟要說明清楚。
・使用表達次序的承轉語，例如 first、then、after that 等使段落連貫。
・你說明的是一般性而非特定一次的過程時，可以不用過去式。

參考範文

lanning a surprise party can be easy. First, you need to decide where and when to have the party and whom to invite. For example, if you want to plan a surprise birthday party for your friend, you'd first need to decide where. For example, you may choose to surprise him at a restaurant with a private party room. Then, you need a date. How about a Saturday, when most people are available? After that, you'd need to decide who should attend, which depends on the space you have for the party. With this decided, you'd need to call the restaurant to reserve space for all the guests on the Saturday of your party. Thankfully, there are free party-invitation websites, so all you need to do is just type in the email addresses of people who are invited, and the website will send the invitations and let you know who has accepted the invitation and who hasn't. With all your steps completed, it's time to enjoy the party.

Activity

1. 假設你要向外國人介紹臺灣有名的甜點或冰品 (例如芒果冰、珍珠奶茶)，請以一段短文寫下製作的步驟。

2. **How to Plan a Trip**
   假設你計畫在假期和同學去旅遊，以一個段落寫出你如何計畫。

3. **The Ways I Reduce Stress**
   你平時如何抒解壓力呢？以一個段落寫出你自己的方法。

4. **How to Stay Healthy**
   以一段文字寫出你平時都是如何保持健康的。

4d
描述人、地、物
Describing a Person/a Place/an Object

4d-1 描述人、地、物時需注意的要點

· 要使讀者能感受到你描寫的情境，必須會使用形容詞或比喻的手法來描繪你的視覺、聽覺、嗅覺、味覺、觸覺以及你心裡的感受。例如：shiny, messy, thundering, fragrant, juicy, smooth, as soft as silk, frustrated, fascinated 等等。

在 *The Secret Garden*《秘密花園》中，作者用生動的比喻描寫知更鳥：...he hopped and flirted his tail and twittered. It was **as if he were talking**. His red waistcoat **was like satin**, and he puffed his tiny breast out and was so fine and so grand and so pretty that it was really **as if he were showing her how important**...。

> **The Secret Garden**
> Frances Burnett

· 描述地點時要注意空間順序。

4d-2 範例

題目

描述一個地方、一個很特別的人或一件很新奇的物品。題目自訂，例如 **A Beautiful Local Park**、**My Friend** 或 **My Favorite Fruit**。

提示

· 第一句就要指出你要描述的對象，以及為什麼要描述。
· 可以多運用描述性質的詞語來描寫感官印象 (你所看到、聽到或感覺到的)。

參考範文

Living in the crowded downtown area of a large city makes me value the park next to my apartment. This quiet, peaceful park takes up an entire city block with its tall trees, artificial creek and colorful flower garden that is planted by downtown residents. When I sit in the park and close my eyes, a variety of sounds can be heard: the bubbling creek, birds chirping and sometimes fighting, and children asking about the flowers as they walk through the park with their parents. In the summer, the trees and grass make the park a rich, dark green. In winter, it's transformed into a sparkling jewel. On winter days, the snow sparkles in the sunlight and I can see my breath as I exhale into the freezing air. At night, though, the white and colored lights in the trees turn on, making for a glowing, colorful sight.

Activity

1. An Interesting Person

介紹一個很有趣的朋友或家人。除了描述此人的外表之外，重點要放在如何有趣，可以舉一些例子來說明。參考以下提示的詞彙：

外表	long and slim legs in shape	broad shoulders dark/blond hair	of average/heavy build curly/straight hair

個性	an introvert/extrovert humorous	sociable/outgoing quick-thinking	shy/withdrawn optimistic

2. A Different Restaurant

寫一段短文介紹一家很特別的餐廳並說明特別之處為何。

3. 假設你是觀光局的員工，你的上司要求你介紹某個觀光景點以吸引外國遊客。請將介紹寫成一段文字 (可以選擇你最熟悉的景點來寫，例如：The Sun Moon Lake、Ken-ting、Mt. Ali)。

4. A Visit to a Night Market

你去過夜市嗎？在那裡你看到什麼？聽到什麼？吃了什麼？

5. 你是不是到過很酷的商店？以 **A Cool Store** 為題，描述這家商店。

4e Giving Reasons　提出理由

4e-1　提出理由時需注意的要點

· 為了要條理分明，說明理由之前一定要先列出大綱來，依照大綱再添加細節說明，組成段落。
· 說明理由時要依照重要順序排列。表列舉的承轉語請參考 3b-2。

4e-2　範例

題目

　　生活中有什麼是你認為很重要的呢？音樂？棒球？上網？請以＿＿＿＿＿ **is Important to Me** 為題說明理由。

提示

· 主題句最簡單的寫法就是：＿＿＿＿＿ is important to me for several reasons.。
· 結論句可以重述主題。

參考範文

Volunteering my time and professional skills is important to me for several reasons. First of all, I feel it is important to contribute to society by helping others. For me, it makes the most sense to do this by offering my writing and public relations services to nonprofit organizations that help others. Volunteering is also important because it makes me feel good that I can help a person or organization that is in need. Furthermore, I have been very lucky in my life and feel it's important to share that good luck with others who may not have an easy life. Last, but not least, volunteering is important to me for business reasons. Companies and clients are always judging the people working for them, and it's important to look good in their eyes. I have gotten a lot of satisfaction from volunteering, and it's important to me for these reasons.

Activity

1. **Why Is English Important?**
   學英文在臺灣幾乎已成了全民運動，舉出理由來說明學英文為什麼重要。

2. **My Favorite Season**
   舉出理由來說明在這個季節裡，有什麼視覺、聽覺、嗅覺上的感受讓你最喜歡。

3. **I (Don't) Like Rainy Days**
   雨天讓你感到清新或厭煩呢？舉出理由說明你為何喜歡或不喜歡雨天。

4. **I'd Like to Have an Interview with...**
   如果你有機會訪談一個名人，這個人可以是你熟悉的國內外明星、科學家或政治人物，也可以是小說或電影中的人物。以一段文字寫出你想訪談哪一個人，並提出理由。

5. **My Favorite Holiday**
   為什麼喜歡這節日，你喜歡做什麼，和誰一起過，舉出理由來說明。

6. **My Favorite Movie**
   簡單說明劇情，重點在說明為什麼喜歡，電影中的哪一部分最讓你感動。

7. **A Song That Means a Lot to Me**
   簡單介紹歌詞的大意，重點在說明理由。

Making a Comparison or Contrast
做比較或對照

4f-1 做比較或對照時需注意的要點

- 先把兩者的異同之處,或者優缺點全部列出來,再經過取捨後擬訂出大綱。比較可以談相同或相異之處,對照就只談相異之處。
- 呈現的方法有兩種:
    1. 整體呈現法 (block method)
       先談有關甲的要點,然後再談乙的要點。
    2. 要點呈現法 (point-by-point method)
       依要點來安排順序,在每一項要點之下各自談論甲、乙,如此才能使段落有次序 (orderly) 而且前後一致 (parallel)。
- 常用的承轉語請參考 3b-2。

4f-2 範例

題目

　　請比較兩個你熟悉的人或星座,例如:**Aries and Pisces: The First and the Last**。

提示

- 列出兩者相同或相異之處後,要取捨,選出比較特別、有趣或好表達的。
- 列出這些要點後再決定它們適合哪一種安排。
- 一般來說比較簡單的呈現方式是 block method,而 on the other hand 就成了這個方法最常用的承轉語。

參考範文

(以第一種方法安排要點，參見 4f-1)

People born under the Aries and Pisces zodiac signs are thought to have very different personalities. Aries are reportedly confident, energetic and enthusiastic. In other words, they are adventurous and passionate people who would probably do well in business. Aries have personalities that are a bit hard-edged and tough. On the other hand, Pisces are thought to be dreamy, romantic, affectionate and honest. These traits would make them good artists, writers, counselors and, most important, wonderful friends. Pisces have a kind personality, highlighted with love and care. With Aries being the first sign of the zodiac and Pisces being the last, it's no surprise that people born under one of the signs are in such contrast to people born under the other sign. Though both Aries and Pisces can be kind and friendly, they just show their feelings through different personalities.

Vocabulary

- Aries [ˈɛrɪz] *n.* 牡羊座
- Pisces [ˈpaɪˌsiz] *n.* 雙魚座

Activity

1. 以 "My two friends are similar/different in two ways." 為主題句擴展成一個段落 (由外表及個性兩方面討論)。

2. 以 "I am different from what I was five years ago." 為主題句寫一段作文，比較現在的你和五年前有何不同。

3. 請比較你現在居住的地方和你去過或住過的地方，找出相似及相異之處，然後寫成一段作文。

4. 你上學的方式可能有不同的選擇。例如走路或騎腳踏車、騎腳踏車或搭公車、搭公車或捷運、家人載或自己搭車等，請你以一段短文比較這兩種選擇。

5. 記得「瞎子摸象」這則古代寓言故事嗎？以下是美國作家桑德堡 (Carl Sandburg) 所寫的一則現代寓言，也和大象有關。讀完之後，比較兩則故事，並寫下感想。

Elephants Are Different to Different People

Wilson and Pilcer and Snack stood before the zoo elephant.

Wilson said, "What is its name? Is it from Asia or Africa? Who feeds it? Is it a he or a she? If it dies, what will they use the bones, the fat, and the hide for? What use is it besides being looked at?"

Pilcer didn't have any questions; he was murmuring to himself, "It's a house by itself. It stands like a bridge across deep water; the face is sad and the eyes are kind; I know elephants are good to babies."

Snack looked up and down and at last said to himself, "He's a tough and strong animal outside. I believe he is as strong inside. I'll bet he must have a strong heart."

Wilson, Pilcer and Snack didn't put up any arguments. They didn't throw anything to each other's faces. They looked at the elephant in three different ways, but they let it go at that. They didn't spoil a sunny Sunday afternoon. "Sunday comes only once a week," they told each other.

Carl Sandburg
(1878～1976)

討論因果

Discussing Cause and Effect

4g-1 討論因果時需注意的要點

· 寫原因的段落時，先在第一句敘述結果，之後再分項來說明原因。

· 寫結果的段落時，先敘述原因，之後再分項來說明結果。

· 為了說明能有條理，一定要先擬訂大綱。

4g-2 範例

題目

　　你觀察到同學之間或社會上有什麼普遍現象，又帶來了什麼問題呢？請以 **The Problems _____ Cause(s)** 為題，寫出你觀察到的現象和問題。

提示

・開門見山，一開始就要指出普遍現象是什麼，之後再分項來探討問題。
・表原因的要點要依照重要順序安排。

參考範文

The popularity of social networking websites has led to potential problems for some teenagers. These websites, such as Myspace.com, are like online meeting places where people of any age can post their personal information, photos, music, artwork and blogs, which are similar to online diaries. As a result, on these websites, there are dangers that teens can face from adults who try to lure teens into sexual relationships (which is against the law). Another danger is identity theft that someone steals your personal information and uses it to pretend he or she is you. Yet another problem is that when blogging on these websites, teens can sometimes get into trouble for posting insulting information or lies about other students or teachers. Therefore, it is important for parents and their teenage children to discuss online safety issues and Internet etiquette.

Activity

1. 以 "School stress affects me greatly." 為主題句擴展成一個段落。

2. **The Effects Computers Have Had on Our Lives**
   現在電腦已經非常普遍了。請寫出電腦對我們的生活造成了什麼影響。

3. **Why Are the Japanese Comics So Popular?**

日本漫畫深受青少年喜愛。試以一段文字說明原因。

4. Arguments between Me and My Parents

你和父母會有衝突嗎？請以一段文字說明引起衝突的原因。

定義字或用語
Defining a Word or a Term

4h-1 定義字或用語時需注意的要點

・段落第一句就要解釋定義，如果可能，盡量使用英英字典裡的定義。
・下定義之後，列舉細節或實例來說明。

以下這些問題提供你構思段落時可以發展的方向。
1. What does this word/term mean?
2. When or in what situations do people use the word or do the activity?
3. How do people use the word or do the activity?
4. Do you like to use the word or to do the activity?
5. Can you give an example that can explain what this word/term mean?

4h-2 範例

題目

現在很多人都感嘆人心越來越貪婪，社會越來越腐化。請以 **Greed** 為題寫一篇作文探討何謂 greed。

提示

- 先解釋 greed 是什麼，再談貪心會有什麼後果。
- 可以舉出實例或是細節來說明。

參考範文

> **G**reed can be the most destructive of emotions. Generally defined as "wanting something you don't need," greed can lead to financial and legal problems for people who can't control themselves. For example, wanting too many things that one doesn't need can lead one to borrow money to buy things, without having the means to pay the money back. Greed also causes people to commit such crimes as fraud and robbery. They steal from either other people or banks. Sadly, the economy of most developed countries is based on greed: the buying and selling of the unneeded or even useless products. Strangely, though, many people are still driven by greed even when they have found that possessions and money do not always lead to happiness.

Vocabulary

- destructive [dɪ`strʌktɪv] *adj.* 毀滅性的
- fraud [frɔd] *n.* [U] 詐欺

Activity

1. 青少年使用了不少流行語，你是否曾經向父母或老師解釋過什麼是機車 (Jihche)？什麼是勁爆 (Jinbao)？把你的解釋寫成一段作文。
2. 任選以下的字或詞下定義，並寫成一段作文。
   (1) friendship　　　　(2) happiness　　　　(3) love
   (4) generation gap　　(5) white lies　　　　(6) a green thumb

表達意見
Expressing an Opinion

4i-1　表達意見時需注意的要點

- 這類文體尤其重視條理清晰、結構嚴謹,因此一定要先擬好大綱,依據大綱寫作。
- 通常段落開始時就提出立場,表明贊成或反對某事,之後再提出理由。
- 要有系統與邏輯,而且要強而有力地提出自己的論點。以下兩個著名的演說詞都是很好的例子:

第二次世界大戰期間,1940 年英法聯軍戰敗,英國首相邱吉爾 (Winston Churchill) 發表演說鼓舞全民奮戰到底,他說:...we shall not flag or fail. We shall go on to the end, ...we shall fight on the seas and oceans, we shall fight with growing confidence and growing strength in the air, we shall defend our Island, whatever the cost may be...。

 另外美國第三十五任總統甘迺迪 (John F. Kennedy) 在 1961 年發表的

就職演說詞中,有兩句至今仍經常被引用:My fellow Americans: ask not what your country can do for you— ask what you can do for your country. My fellow citizens of the world: ask not what America will do for you, but what together we can do for the freedom of man.。

- 可以運用的技巧包括提出例子、引用研究證明或統計數字、引用權威人士的言論來支持自己的看法,或者運用有力的邏輯推論。
- 在段落結尾時,通常會重申立場。

4i-2 範例

題目

　　據報導，每年約有一千七百萬隻動物被用來做醫學研究的實驗，你對此事的看法如何？請以 **Do We Have the Right to Use Animals in Medical Research?** 為題寫出你的看法。

提示

- 第一句：先陳述這項事實。
- 第二句：提出反方看法 (有人質疑人類是否有此權利)。
- 第三句：以 "In my opinion, ..." 開始寫出你的看法。

參考範文

　　　Every year about seventeen million of animals are used in laboratory experiments. In many countries today, some people are starting to ask a question: Do we have the right to use animals this way? In my opinion, we have every reason to use animals in medical research. The use of animals in medical research actually has many practical benefits. Animal research has enabled researchers to develop treatment for many diseases, such as heart disease and depression. It would not have been possible to develop vaccines for diseases like smallpox and polio without animal research. Every drug anyone takes today was tried first on animals. Is the life of a rat more important than a three-year-old child? Absolutely not. What's more, it is reported that last year over twelve million animals had to be killed in animal shelters because nobody wanted them as pets. Medical research, as a result, is an excellent way of using these unwanted animals. There can be no doubt that human beings have the right to use animals in medical research.

> • vaccine [ˋvæksɪn] *n.* [U] [C] 疫苗
> • smallpox [ˋsmɔl͵pɑks] *n.* [U]【醫】天花
> • polio [ˋpolɪ͵o] *n.* [U]【醫】小兒麻痺 (=poliomyelitis)

Activity

1. 請模仿以上範文的結構，以下列的主題句和要點擴展成段落。

Topic Sentence: I don't agree with the idea about using animals in medical research.

Point 1: the same rights as humans have

Point 2: cruelty

Point 3: better ways to do the research

2. **Should High School Students Wear Uniforms?**

你贊成或反對中學生穿制服呢？寫出你的看法。

3. 假設你要去聽現場演唱會，而你父母認為在家看電視轉播就可以了。以一段文字說服你父母讓你去享受現場表演。

4. 有些父母禁止孩子去網咖，有些父母准許，你的看法呢？

5. 假設你父母是很反對使用電腦的人，寫一段短文說服父母使用電腦會如何讓生活更方便。

6. 有人強調學生只需要專心唸書，不必關心任何發生在你四周的事，你的看法呢？

■寫一個段落的作文會不會太長了？可不可以分段？

　　把 120～150 字的作文寫成一段絕對不嫌長。如果你一定要分段，可以把主題句擴展成類似 Essay 結構中的 Introduction，成為第一段，但最多只能寫兩三句，千萬不可話說從頭，佔了太多篇幅。支持句和結論就一起放在第二段。以第一章 Teacher's Note 中的參考作文為例，可以從 "Whenever I am extremely bored...." 這一句開始分段。

■寫作文一定要先打草稿嗎？之後要如何修正呢？

　　原則上，寫作文必須依循大綱來打草稿。之後再依照下列幾項要點來檢視你的作文是否需要修正：
1. 段落有主題句，主題句包含有主題論述 (controlling idea)。
2. 主題句之後的句子 (也就是支持句) 能充分地闡明主題。
3. 段落中所有的句子都與主題有關，而且有一定的邏輯次序。
4. 使用適當的承轉語，使文章的語氣連貫。
5. 有結論句，讓作文有個收尾，才有完整性。
　　在你交出作文之前，還有一件工作很重要：檢查是否有標點符號、拼字、文法或句子結構方面的錯誤。

■考試時哪有時間打草稿呢？

　　考試的時候你只有二十到三十分鐘的時間寫作文，的確沒有時間先寫草稿再慢慢修正。我的建議是把寫作練習分成兩個階段：
1. 在高二到高三上學期這段時間，寫作文時要先有草稿再修正，熟練到一篇好文章應有的條件已經在你腦子裡根深蒂固了。
2. 到了考前兩三個月，你可以練習不寫草稿，直接依照大綱來寫，但是要把大綱的要點和細節寫得仔細一些，例如在寫第一章中，Teacher's Note 裡的範例文章之前，就可以擬出這樣的大綱：Point 1: a friend to be with when I am bored (touch the keys; melody comes into mind; play games with me)，之後你只要把這些關鍵字寫成句子就可以了。

NOTE ▶▶▶

Essay Writing
短文寫作

▶ Essay 通常是指包含三段以上的文章。其結構通常可分成引言、主體和結論這三個部分。另外，以下就最常見的文體（敘述文、描寫文、因果文、比較或對照文與議論文）來練習寫作。

5a
引言
Introduction

5a-1 引言的功能

· 引起讀者閱讀的興趣。
· 提供讀者文章內容的重點 (即主旨)。

5a-2 引言的兩個主要部分

· 主題導引 (lead-in)：
  就是開場白，提供背景資料，運用一些技巧來引起閱讀動機。一般高中生的作文可以寫 1 到 2 句。
· 主題論述 (thesis statement)：
  其功能就像是段落的主題句，所不同三處是主題句呈現段落的主旨，而主題論述陳述的是文章的主旨，通常在引言的最後一句。

LOOK

主題句→呈現段落的主旨。
主題論述→呈現全文的主旨。尤其在說明文及議論文中，主題論述是非常重要的。

5a-3 引言的寫法

- 寫主題導引時可運用以下技巧來達到吸引注意力的目的：
  (1) 驚人的訊息或事實
  (2) 問句
  (3) 引用語 (專家、名人的話或諺語等)
  (4) 統計數字
  (5) 小故事或背景資料
- 主題論述的寫法與注意事項和主題句相同，請參考 2b。

　　以下的範例將說明主題導引運用的技巧，以及如何導入主題 (主題論述的句子以粗體標示)。

範例

(1)

　　　1 Would you ever eat live cockroaches or worms?　2 Do you dare to swim with sharks or let someone give you an electric shock?　3 Recently on some new "extreme" TV shows, many people do have these experiences.　4 **Over the past few years, extreme TV shows have become some of the most popular programs on television.**

說明 運用問句和驚人的訊息兩種技巧：

　　第 1～2 句→用令人難以置信的問句來引起注意。

　　第 3 句→就像一座橋，將內容導至明確的主題 (extreme TV shows)。

(2)

　　　1 Sometimes most of us find that we forget where we placed our cell phones.　2 Sometimes we are trying to remember a name, but it is on the tip of our tongue.　3 Now experts say, "We are not helpless in the face of failing memory."　4 **Here are two different ways—physical and mental—to keep our memory fresh.**

說明 運用背景資料和引用語兩種技巧：

　　第 1～2 句→提供和生活相關的背景資料。

　　第 3 句→引用專家的話來導入正題 (not helpless...failing memory)。

(3)

　　1 Although shopping is delightful, it can also be exhausting. 2 Today, however, the Internet has made this tiring activity more convenient. 3 **Online shopping is one of the biggest success stories.**

說明 運用背景資料的技巧：

第 1 句→提到「購物雖然令人愉悅，但也很耗費心力」這項背景資料。

第 2 句→聚焦至網路購物，呈現了主題，為第 3 句的主題論述作準備。

(4)

　　1 In the United States many people enjoy eating oversized sandwiches for lunch. 2 However, did you know that in America, a sandwich is not always a sandwich? 3 **Depending on the region of the country you are in, the oversized sandwich is called by a different name.**

說明 運用背景資料和問句的技巧。

第 1 句→提到美國人中餐喜歡吃超大三明治。

第 2 句→以問句 (Did you know that...a sandwich is not always a sandwich?) 來導入正題。

5b 主體
Body

5b-1　撰寫主體的注意事項

1. 可以視需要分成幾個段落。以 1950 年諾貝爾文學獎得主羅素的作品 "What I Have Lived For" 為例，主體分成三段是因為引言提到 three passions——the longing for love, the search for knowledge, and unbearable pity for the suffering of mankind，因此將主體分成三段。

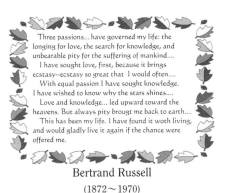

Three passions... have governed my life: the longing for love, the search for knowledge, and unbearable pity for the suffering of mankind....
　　I have sought love, first, because it brings ecstasy--ecstasy so great that I would often....
　　With equal passion I have sought knowledge. I have wished to know why the stars shines....
　　Love and knowledge... led upward toward the heavens. But always pity brougt me back to earth....
　　This has been my life. I have found it woth living, and would gladly live it again if the chance were offered me.

Bertrand Russell
(1872～1970)

2. 每個段落要闡明一個中心思想，這個中心思想通常出現在段落的主題句。
   主題句必須跟隨著引言的指示走 ， 也就是必須根據引言的主題論述來寫 topic
   sentences。
3. 至於段落怎麼寫和第二章所介紹的段落寫作技巧是相同的 。 可以參考 2c
   Supporting Sentences。
4. 段落與段落之間可以使用代名詞、重述前段的字或要點，或者用承轉語使文氣連
   貫。

   以下範例說明段落與段落之間如何連貫的技巧：

(1)

　　...It is displayed in the children they teach, and, with talent and persistence,
a good teacher can create a masterpiece.

　　To accomplish **this**, a teacher must realize that there is more to teach than
simply to help students to achieve high grades....

說明 第二個段落使用代名詞達成段落間的連貫。

(2)

　　Some 20th-century chairs are made of steel. **The material was undreamed
of in the 18th century.**

　　Steel was developed by engineers in the 19th century. Because of its
strength, steel soon became a useful building material....

說明 第二段承接上一段的方式是 ： 第一句以不同的文字內容重述與第一段最後
　　 一句語意類似的話。

(3)

A. **In contrast**, Switzerland will never need to fight lateness in this way, as the
   Swiss are famous for punctuality....

B. **However**, many children miss out on this important daily meal. A large
   number of parents say they are too busy to sit down and eat breakfast with
   their children....

說明 這兩個段落第一句都用了承轉語來連貫語氣。

5c   結論

Conclusion

5c-1   撰寫結論的注意事項

1. 必須簡潔有力，大約兩個或三個句子即可。
2. 撰寫結論的方法有以下幾種：(可參考 2d)
    (1) 重述主旨：需注意用字遣詞要再調整
        Thesis statement:
        There are different ideas about pets in different parts of the world.
        Conclusion:
        Pets around the world live in a great variety of ways, just as people do.
    (2) 提出呼籲、建議或預測未來

    範例
    (A)
        This trip was fantastic.   2 So when there are holidays, get packed and head for Taitung to enjoy the marvelous scenery.
        說明 第二句呼籲讀者也去臺東一遊。

    (B)
        1 How long will extreme TV shows stay popular?   2 No one knows, but some fear that new extreme TV shows will have even more outrageous and shocking stunts.   3 In the future, extreme TV shows may become even more extreme.
        說明 第三句為對未來提出預告。
    (3) 下結論：這種技巧常用在議論文中

    範例
        On the whole, nowadays we human beings cannot stop using animals for medical research, but I believe that with the advance in biological

science, in the near future researchers can find other ways of doing the research.

說明 作者在一番論述之後提出了結論：現在不可能停止用動物做實驗，但將來會找到其他做實驗的方法。

Narrative Essays 敘述文

敘述文是敘述經歷或事件發生的過程，包括故事、小說、生活趣事、介紹電影情節等。另外在日常生活中，許多談話的內容也具有敘述的性質，例如和朋友分享自己經歷的趣事等。

5d-1  寫敘述文的原則及技巧

1. 引言要能吸引讀者

既然是敘述故事，引言就要能吸引讀者，讓讀者心中產生疑問。例如是誰 (Who)？在什麼時間 (When)？去了什麼地方 (Where)？發生什麼事 (What)？怎麼發生的 (How)？為什麼 (Why)？

2. 內容需切中要點

敘述時要能回答讀者心中的問題，上面提到的六項就是敘述文的要素。

3. 敘述時要篩選重點

敘述的內容不要太瑣碎，不可把所有發生的細節一一寫下來，要篩選出重要情節。就像你敘述學校發生的趣事給家人聽的時候，也要捨去一些細節，只保留重點。

4. 事件要有連貫性

敘述時要特別注意流暢度，也就是連貫性，否則會影響閱讀。

5. 多運用描寫的技巧

在敘述過程中要運用描寫的技巧，例如：看到大海的感覺、聽到蟲鳴鳥叫、聞到花的香氣等，這些文字讓敘述文更生動。

6. 善用對話

運用人物的對話，有時候比文字的描寫更能使人物更生動。1954 年的諾貝爾文學獎得主海明威 (Ernest Hemingway)，就是運用對話呈現聲音意象的高手。他的短篇小說 "The Killers" 幾乎是對話的組合。寫對話時要把人物所說的話放在引號 (" ") 中。

"What are you looking at?" Max looked at George.
"Nothing."
"The hell you were. You were looking at me."
"Maybe the boy meant it for a joke, Max," Al said. George laughed.

5d-2　敘述文引言的寫法

· 在背景資料中提出場景、人物或是預告，來吸引讀者的好奇心。
· 敘述文主旨並不像其他文體那麼明確，所以主題論述的寫法就會不同：
 (1) 可以沒有主旨，只是為主體的故事發展起個頭。例如下一段要寫夢境，引言最後一句可以寫 "I was so tired from shopping that I fell asleep almost immediately."。
 (2) 可以說出從事件得到的教訓，或提出寓意作為文章主旨。也可以讓讀者保有新鮮感，保留到在結論部分再提出這個主旨。

引言範例

以下是題目為 **An Important Event** 的引言範例。

> The annual school dance was a big event, but I had not attended my new school for long, so I really didn't want to go. I hadn't made any friends, and I knew I would spend the whole evening feeling left out on the sidelines. My mother, however, refused to let me miss it.

說明 作者提出的主題是她不想參加的 school dance，引起讀者好奇後來會發生什麼事情。

5d-3　敘述文主體的寫法

· 情節的安排一定要按照時間順序。
· 主體的分段要有整體性，不能凌亂。例如：可以安排為開始、中間和結尾三段，依時間順序或者是依地點來分。

· 要注意段與段之間的連貫性。

主體範例

But I can't argue with my mom. So Friday evening arrived, and there I was in the school hall, sitting on a chair and trying not to catch the eye of any of my teachers. I knew they'd feel sorry for me and probably come over, and then I'd have no chance of talking to anyone my own age for the rest of the night. The hall had been decorated, and a DJ was playing music. Some kids were dancing, and others were sitting down like me, but in groups, talking non-stop.

I was gazing into space and telling myself that I didn't mind being on my own when I heard a loud "Hey!" in my ear. It was Carol, a girl from my class.

"Are you having fun?" she asked.

"Yes," I said. "I'm having a great time." I hoped that she didn't hear the self-pity in my voice.

She looked at me doubtfully for a second, and then said, "Come and sit with us."

I frowned, afraid that she was only being nice because she felt sorry for me, but she went on, "Please come. The others dared me to ask you."

"Why?" I asked.

"Everyone else is scared of you! You always look like you don't want to talk to anyone," she said.

I could hardly believe my ears, but I decided to play it cool. I smiled, and said, "Of course, I'll come." The rest of the night went by quickly, as I talked and laughed and danced. I had a great time!

說明

· 主體共分為開始 (第一段)、中間 (第二段以及所有的對話段落) 以及結束 (最後一段)。

· 第一段點出舞會舉行的時間和地點,並描述場景和作者的心情。中間的段落一開始就提出了關鍵人物 Carol,並且運用對話來描述心境轉變的過程。最後一段則敘述轉變的結果。

5d-4　敘述文結論的寫法

常用的方法有兩種：

· 提出從事件學到的經驗或教訓，或者提出事件造成的結果，例如："I learned from the accident that honesty is the best policy." 或 "Now I am more careful with my money."。

· 提出對未來的預測，例如："I'll never sit up and watch baseball games again."。

結論範例

So, my mom was right after all. That night changed my life because I hadn't realized how unapproachable my loneliness had made me. If I hadn't gone to the dance, I would have missed a chance to make some friends.

說明 提出母親來和引言段落相呼應，並且敘述此事件造成的結果 (changed my life)。

寫敘述文時可以多運用明喻和暗喻的技巧。另外切記不要只侷限在視覺上的描寫 (可參考 5e-1)。

5d-5　寫作練習

1. 以 **A Summer/Winter Trip to** ＿＿＿＿＿為題，敘述一次旅遊的過程。

參考範文

We stepped off the plane from Christchurch on to a frozen runway. The surrounding mountains were covered in snow and the air was cold and crisp. It was minus five degrees. Queenstown, at the south-west of New Zealand's South

Island, is the country's Adventure Capital. In summer it attracts action-seekers who come to bungee-jump off high bridges, parachute off tall peaks and jet-boat along swift rocky rivers. Luckily we had arrived in winter so we planned to ski and snowboard every day, and we were going to party all night long as well because it was Winter Festival Week. Every year during this noisy week Queenstown goes crazy, with visiting jazz and rock bands, and floodlit skiing well into the evening.

Queenstown sits beside Lake Wakatipu, one of New Zealand's many deep lakes. Tall mountains rise from the lake on all sides and there is a spectacular view from almost every window in town. We checked into our hotel, and then headed straight for the ski slopes. We were excited to finally be up in the snow, as we waited to get our skis and snowboards fitted. Our hands and feet tingled with the cold and we shivered till we got moving. After a quick ski lesson we were soon racing down the slopes like everyone else. That night, exhausted, we all gathered at Winnie's Bar for pizza and a few drinks. A big log fire warmed our tired bodies as we shared funny ski stories.

The days that followed were a rush of exciting new ski runs, sore muscles, snow-burnt skin and steaming cups of espresso coffee. Each night we visited a new café or bar, or ordered take-out to eat in our rooms, and during the day we raced up and down the mountain, thrilled at our new-found skills on skis. During winter Queenstown is full of young people from around the world who come to join the skiing and the festival, and to try some of the other exciting adventure activities in the area. Like them, we tried a bit of everything.

All too soon our time was up and we headed to the airport for our flight back to Christchurch. As our plane took off it zigzagged between the snowy mountains before gaining a higher altitude. Out the window we could see skiers racing down the slopes of Coronet Peak, reminding us of a great week in the snow.

2. 請以 **My Most Embarrassing Experience** 為題，寫一篇文章。敘述一個讓你感到最尷尬的時刻。

3. 將 4a 的 Activity 第 3 題，「敘述你最喜歡的一部電影的情節」這篇段落作文，改寫為主體至少有兩個段落的文章。

4. 以 **A Touching Story** 為題，寫出你聽過的一則令你感動的故事。

5. 回想一下哪一次生日最難忘或最特別，然後以 **My Best／Unforgettable Birthday** 為題，寫出那次過生日的過程。

描寫文
Descriptive Essays

　　描寫文是一幅文字圖畫。用生動的文字描繪人、地、物的細節，讓讀者心中浮現栩栩如生的畫面，是描寫文的目的。描寫文體經常會出現在敘述文中，使得人物與場景更活潑生動。

5e-1　寫描寫文的原則及技巧

1. 要選擇一個描寫的觀點或角度
例如可以從客觀角度談朋友的外表或家庭背景，也可以主觀地談個性、嗜好或你對他的情感。

2. 決定最想凸顯的主題，呈現出一個主要印象
例如你要描寫 KTV 唱歌的情景，要抓住一個主要印象，是歡樂還是吵雜呢？如此文章才能聚焦。

3. 找出很特別的或者令人印象深刻的細節要點
例如你要描寫狗的忠誠，就可以從牠平日的行為中挑選出最具代表性的例子來描寫。

4. 按照空間或時間順序描寫

5. 描寫要生動與形象鮮明
大家熟知的一本童話書 *The Little Prince*《小王子》，其中描述種子發芽的兩個句子就非常生動：They (the seeds)

The Little Prince
Antoine de Saint Exupéry

sleep deep in the heart of the earth's darkness, until someone among them is seized with the desire to awaken. Then this little seed will stretch itself and begin—timidly at first—to push a charming little sprig inoffensively upward toward the sun.。

形象生動鮮明的描寫有兩個常用的方法：

(1) 善用不同感官來描寫景物的手法，包括聽覺的、嗅覺的、觸覺的或味覺的描寫，而非只述說眼睛所見的，例如：

- The doorknob turned slowly and with a rusty groan the door began to open.

  → turned slowly 和 open 是眼睛所見的，但加了 a rusty groan 就好像聽到了聲音，更為生動。

- I lay on the hilltop, staring at the sky and listening to the leaves of the pine tree rustling in the soothing breeze. →聽覺的描寫

- The chocolate tastes exceptionally smooth and creamy. →味覺的描寫

- My hands feel like sandpaper in the winter, and hand cream doesn't help. →觸覺的描寫

- The weather is beautiful. The sun is shining, and the white clouds are marshmallow-puffy. →觸覺的描寫

- Delicious smell of roasting sweet corn lasted all day in my room. →嗅覺的描寫

- The sounds of the night market filled the air. Vendors shouted out bargains to draw the crowd from their competitors. The sounds of feet strolling across the street and conversations about what to buy filled the streets and floated into nearby shops and apartments. →聽覺的描寫

(2) 善用比喻的手法

a. 明喻 (simile)

把描寫的對象比喻做另一個類似而熟悉的事物。會使用 as、like、as if 和 as...as 等比喻詞。

- You are like the sun.
- Lucy is as quiet as a mouse.
- The water in the pool is as clear as crystal.
- She waited in a corner by herself, continually glancing at her watch as if

she were waiting for someone to join her.
- Jane and Iris had their heads together, like two people sharing a secret.
- My love for you is like an ocean, and cannot be erased.
- Snowflakes shine like silver butterflies drifting in the sky.
- Advice is like snow. The softer it falls, the longer it dwells upon and the deeper it sinks into the mind.

b. 隱喻 (metaphor)

不使用比喻詞的比喻方式，在詩或歌詞中很常見。

- You are my sunshine.
- You are such a mule.
- You are a cunning old fox.
- You are a sheep, always following others.
- Your comment added fuel to the fire.
- Laughter is the sun that drives winter from the human face.

5e-2 描寫文引言的寫法

1. 段落一開始就提出和描寫對象的關係，包括何時去過這地方、此人是誰或此物何時擁有。之後為了引起興趣可以加上一句，例如：
   - I can't wait to eat at this restaurant again.
   - The Grand Haven State Park beach is a wonderful place.
   - I will always cherish it in my lifetime.
2. 用一個句子寫出描繪主題的感覺。例如：
   - The restaurant has a warm and family-friendly atmosphere as well as delicious treats.
   - The beautiful scenes of a summer sunset on Lake Michigan often appear in my dream.

引言範例

以下是題目為 **A Great Place to Go** 的文章範例。

There are several beautiful west coast beaches just 30 minutes' drive from where I live in Auckland, New Zealand's largest city. When friends from overseas come to stay, I take them to Piha. This wild beach is a great place to go because it is uniquely New Zealand.

說明

1. 背景資料提出了這地方在哪裡,以及和作者是什麼關係。

2. 最後一個句子中提出作者的感覺:很野 (wild) 以及很紐西蘭 (uniquely New Zealand)。

5e-3 描寫文主體的寫法

這部分就是要用具體的細節來描繪主題。如果主題是餐廳的食物和氣氛,就可以分兩段來描寫;如果讓你難忘的地點除了景色之外,還有一同賞景的人,也可以分成這兩段。記住,運用文字語言的魔力把細節描繪得生動逼真。

描寫文的段落不一定要有主題句。

主體範例

Piha is a wild, windswept beach. It has black sand, which makes it look very different from the white sand beaches of tropical islands. An enormous rock sits in the middle of the beach. It's called Lion Rock, named for the fact that it looks like an enormous lion lying on the sand. The surf booms endlessly as the big waves roll into shore. It's a place that can make you feel very lonely, even though there are always other people around. On the other hand, you feel exhilarated by the power of the waves and the wind, too.

There are plenty of things to do there. Most people go to Piha to swim or surf. Piha is New Zealand's most famous surf beach. Championship surfing competitions are held here, and surfers go out to ride the waves all year round. There is a strong Surf Lifesaving Club, whose members patrol the beach during the summer. Piha has rips and strong currents, so it is dangerous to swim here, unless you swim between the lifesavers' flags. Fishing off the rocks is also dangerous because of the big waves, but that does not stop people from doing it. Besides these exciting activities, people can ride horses along the beach, and there are many great walking tracks through the native rainforest that surrounds Piha.

說明

1. 第一段寫景，包括海灘、岩石、大浪還有很奇妙的氛圍 (讓人寂寞又興奮)。
2. 第二段描述遊客在此可以做的事很多樣化。

5e-4 描寫文結論的寫法

最簡單的方式是將前述的細節做個摘要，或者再次強調對人、地、物的印象，與引言呼應。

結論範例

Swimming and surfing always give you an appetite, and it is traditional to buy fish and chips and eat them on the beach before going home. A visit to Piha makes New Zealanders feel proud of their country, and it shows tourists something of the real New Zealand.

說明 第一句提出回家前吃 fish and chips，這是補充海灘的特色。第二句 something of the real New Zealand 和引言相呼應。

5e-5 寫作練習

1. 請以 **My Favorite Singer/Artist/Actor/Actress** 為題寫一篇描寫文，你可以描述他／她們的作品，並說明喜愛的原因。

參考範文

My Favorite Singer

My favorite singer is definitely Ani DiFranco. I first heard her singing on a student radio station while I was driving my car to my university. The words in her songs were so powerful that I went and bought her CD the next day.

Ani DiFranco's music covers all sorts of political and social issues, especially feminism. Her song "Not a Pretty Girl" is a perfect example of this. It challenges stereotypes of beauty, myths about femininity, and the role of women in the world. Other songs look at equality in relationships and how women are treated by figures of authority, such as the police. Ani DiFranco's music has had such an impact on feminism that the U.S. National Organization of Women (N.O.W.) has recognized her work by awarding her their "woman of courage" prize.

Her music discusses other issues as well. She writes about the power structures of governments, corporations, and the way we treat the environment and one another. A good example of this is her latest album, called "Reprieve". The songs on this album were inspired by the impact of Hurricane Katrina on the people of New Orleans and by her anger at the politics of the Bush Administration.

Ani DiFranco does not look like your typical pop star. Over the years her looks have changed quite a lot, but they have always been unusual. She has sported long dreadlocks, multicolored hair and a shaved head. These adventurous hairstyles suit her personality, which is anything but conservative!

I believe that it is important to listen to music that is powerful and challenging as well as entertaining. Ani DiFranco's music, her words and her ideas caught my attention straight away and her songs have changed the way that I look at parts of life. She challenges me and makes me think. That is why Ani DiFranco is my favorite musician.

> • feminism [ˋfɛmənɪzəm] *n.* [U] 女性主義
> • administration [ədˌmɪnəˋstreʃən] *n.* [C] 政府
> • dreadlocks [ˋdrɛdˌlɑks] *n. pl.* 長髮綹

2. 寫一篇文章描述你熟悉的人物。除了對人物的描寫之外，還可以描述你與他之間的互動過程，或者喜愛他、敬愛他的理由。建議的題目是：

   (1) A Person I Admire Most

   (2) My Favorite Family Member

   (3) My Favorite Actor/Actress

3. 寫一篇文章描述你去過的地方。除了描寫地方之外，還要說出它的特色。建議的題目是：

   (1) A Place I Can Relax

   (2) A Fun Place in the City/Town I Live

   (3) The Most Beautiful Scenic Spot in Taiwan

5f　Cause and Effect Essays　因果文

　　因果文呈現的是原因和結果之間的關係。它分析或討論某個現象或行為是由什麼原因造成的，或者是會造成什麼結果。因果文主要可分為分析原因和討論結果兩種：

(1) 分析原因

　　先呈現果 (例如青少年的壓力)，然後分析造成這個現象的原因。

Cause 1: heavy schoolwork

Cause 2: problems with friends ⟶ Effect: teen stress

Cause 3: parental pressure

(2) 討論結果

　　先呈現因 (例如青少年的壓力)，然後討論會造成的結果。

Effect 1: anxiety

Cause: teen stress → Effect 2: physical illness

Effect 3: withdrawal

5f-1　寫因果文的原則及技巧

1. 在構思階段，畫構思圖 (參考 1a-2) 是很好的選擇，藉這個方法可以刪去次要的部分，只呈現最主要的原因和結果。
2. 呈現原因和結果時，運用細節和舉例說明是很好的方法。
3. 因果文中承轉語的運用特別重要，能讓因果之間的邏輯關係非常清楚 (參考 3b-2)。

5f-2　因果文引言的寫法

- 主題導引：提供相關的背景資料或是觀察到的現象。
- 主題陳述：提出要分析或討論的主要因或果，或者只是很概括的說 "There are three reasons for/theories about/effects of...."、"There are three reasons why...." 或 "...has had three effects on...." 等。而因或果則留到主體討論。

引言範例

　　以下是題目為 **Professional Soccer is Popular Worldwide, But Not in America** 的引言範例。

> Professional soccer is considered by many people to be the most popular spectator sport in the world. Despite the game's worldwide popularity, however, soccer is not a popular spectator sport in America. This is curious when one considers that soccer is the second-most popular team sport for American elementary school students. There are three theories, though, about why professional soccer never really catches on in America.

說明

1. 前三句提供背景資料，也提出了 professional soccer is not popular in America 的

觀察。第三句則為下一句主題陳述做準備。

2. 第四句為主題陳述，只是指出有 three theories。

5f-3　因果文主體的寫法

・一個段落只談一個因或一個果，依此分段。

・因果文是說明文的一種，每一個段落最好都要有主題句。

・因果的要點安排要依照重要性順序。

主體範例

One theory for soccer's lack of popularity is that Americans are too interested in watching basketball, hockey, American football and baseball to have an interest in soccer. The seasons and schedules for these four professional sports are set up so a person could follow two types of games per season, without missing out on the other games. Because of their interest in these other games, most people just don't have the time to watch or money to go to professional soccer games.

Another reason is that Americans—like people from other countries—want to watch star sports players from their country play for their country's team. However, highly talented American soccer players are often recruited to foreign

[rɪˋkrut] *vt.* 招募

teams because they pay a lot more money than American teams. With the best American soccer players joining teams overseas, there are relatively few high-skilled teams in the U.S., which don't draw much interest from the population.

One last theory for the lack of popularity of professional soccer in the United States is that many people consider the sport boring. Some reasons are that "nothing really happens;" not enough goals are scored and too many games end in a tie. One must keep in mind that these comments are made in comparison to such higher-scoring games as American football, basketball and baseball.

說明
每一個主體段落談一個說法。分段清楚，也都有主題句 (第一句)。

5f-4 因果文結論的寫法

· 將因果的要點做個摘要。
· 最後做個總結，或是提出預測或警告。

結論範例

> In conclusion, soccer remains a very popular sport for youth and amateur teams, but most Americans are not willing to pay money to go to a professional soccer game. In fact, there are not even very many professional soccer teams in America, and most Americams dont't pay any attention to them.

說明 這兩句將文章內容做了總結。

5f-5 寫作練習

1. 我們的生活受網路的影響越來越大。請以 **How the Internet Has Quietly Changed Our Lives** 為題，寫一篇文章，討論網路如何改變了我們的生活 (在和過去做比較時，你還會用到比較文的技巧)。

參考範文

> There are many ways in which the Internet has changed our everyday lives. We can keep in contact with friends and relatives in distant places, and find out the latest news as it happens. Perhaps the most important difference is how much time it has quietly saved us, in a variety of ways.
>
> First, imagine you are talking with friends one evening, and you disagree on a fact or figure. Once, you might have had to

spend hours in a library or bookshop to find the right answer. But now, after searching on the Internet for five minutes, you're sure to have it.

Or perhaps your'e too busy to go grocery shopping, or you're sick at home with no food in the fridge. In the past, you would nevertheless have to struggle to the shops to buy groceries. Now, you can simply order online and someone will deliver them. This saves valuable time during a busy day, or allows you to spend more time warm and comfortable if you're sick.

Last, maybe you want to go on vacation, but don't know where. You need to research a destination, check out hotels, then book a plane ticket and possibly rent a car. How would you have done all this without the Internet? You would have had to consult guidebooks, call hotels and travel agents and locate car rental companies. Today, instead, you can do everything on the Internet, making it possible to decide to go on vacation one evening, and leave the next morning with everything arranged in advance. Think how much extra time you save that way, which you can use to enjoy yourself on vacation!

It's clear how, in many different ways, using the Internet can make your use of time much more efficient. But remember, that's only if you use it responsibly. If you spend too long playing online games, downloading songs or movies, or chatting in chat rooms, you might find that the Internet has a rather different effect on your life: instead of more time to spare, you'll actually have no time left for anything else at all.

2. 請以 **The Effects Comic Books/TV Programs/Computer Games Have Had on My Life** 為題，寫出它們對你生活的影響。

3. 請以 **The Reasons Why Cell Phones Are Needed** 為題，說明為什麼需要行動電話 (可參考 1a-2 Activity 2 的構思圖)。

4. 在學校裡你參加什麼社團呢？請以 **Why Should We Join a School Club?** 為題，寫一篇作文，說明中學生為何要參加社團。

5g 比較或對照文
Comparison or Contrast Essays

1. 嚴格來說，compare 是比較相似點，而 contrast 則是比較相異點。
2. 比較或對照這種文體可以比較兩者之間的：
   a. 相似之處
   b. 相異之處
   c. 同時比較相似和相異之處
3. 除了比較異同之外，還可以比較優點或缺點、好處或壞處等等。

5g-1 寫比較或對照文的原則及技巧

・在構思活動中，收集資料後要經過篩選，找出比較重要或有趣的異同處來寫。
・足夠的細節或例子可以使說明更有說服力。
・寫作之前一定要先訂大綱。如此才能避免結構鬆散，失去文章的重點。

5g-2 比較或對照文引言部分的寫法

    引言除了先提供背景資料，指出被比較的人、事或物之外，通常會有一些固定的用法來呈現 thesis statement，例如：

・ Taipei is very much different from what it was thirty years ago in three ways.
・ There are several differences/similarities between my math teacher and English teacher.
・ My father and my mother have different personalities and different attitudes to life.
・ Living in a big city has more advantages than living in the country.
・ My sister and I have several things in common.
・ My father and I share many similarities, but we also have several differences.

引言範例

　　以下是題目為 **The City Versus the Countryside** 的引言範例。

> 　　City life and country life are two very different things. Depending upon where people grow up, their views of the city or the country may be either positive or negative about each of them.

說明 第一句提出要比較的對象，第二句是主題陳述，點出主題要討論的是正面和負面兩種看法。

5g-3 比較或對照文主體的寫法

　　寫主體部分可以有兩種不同的架構：整體呈現法 (block method) 和要點呈現法 (point-by-point method)。那麼該選擇哪一種方法來寫呢？首先要看你比較擅長哪一種寫法。再者，要看哪一種方法比較能清楚呈現你的資料，讓讀者易懂。

• 整體呈現法：

(1) 先談甲方再談乙方，例如要談家人：

主體第一段 → Father $\begin{cases} \text{personality} \\ \text{attitude to life} \end{cases}$

主體第二段 → Mother $\begin{cases} \text{personality} \\ \text{attitude to life} \end{cases}$

(2) 先談甲乙雙方的相似點，再談相異點，例如：

主體第一段→ similarities between me and my sister

主體第二段→ differences between me and my sister

• 要點呈現法：

依要點來安排順序，在每一項要點之下分別談論甲方及乙方，例如：

主體第一段 → personality $\begin{cases} \text{Father} \\ \text{Mother} \end{cases}$

主體第二段 → attitude to life $\begin{cases} \text{Father} \\ \text{Mother} \end{cases}$

主體範例

There are many benefits of living in a big city. First, cities hold many resources that are not available out in the countryside. Large amounts of stores and public transportation make cities very convenient places to live. Since they are population centers, they tend to have many cultural activities that people can experience. People can go and have a good time in theaters, museums and concert halls. As well, universities are often located in big cities, along with large hospitals that offer the best health care.

However, because of the population, there is often a higher crime rate in cities. There is also pollution in different forms, from simple litter on the streets to air, noise, and light pollution. All of these things must be endured on a daily basis for those who choose city life.

Life in the country is much quieter than in the city. People living there can enjoy being closer to nature, and breathe air that is cleaner. The pace of life is often slower, so the hustle and bustle of the big city is not seen. Because the population is more spread out, many of the pollution problems found in cities don't exist. With the clean air and fewer lights constantly lit up, out in the countryside people can see the stars at night.

Yet people are often drawn away from the countryside because there isn't enough opportunity. Jobs are harder to find, and many of the ones available may not be very inviting to a lot of people, such as farming. For people who want to raise a family, many are forced to move to cities where there are better job opportunities.

說明

1. 這是整體呈現的寫法：先談 living in a big city 再談 life in the country。

2. 因為有段落太長的顧慮，所以第一段談住大都市的優點，第二段談缺點。第三段談住鄉村的優點，第四段談缺點 (也可以安排為一段談大都市的優缺點，另一段談鄉村的優缺點)。

3. 在段落與段落之間用適當的承轉語，例如第二段的 However 與第四段的 Yet，使得讀者很清楚語氣轉換了，要談的內容要點會和前一段不同。

5g-4 比較或對照文結論的寫法

　　此部分的寫法大致和其他文體相同。比較不同的是這類文體中,作者通常會對比較的雙方提出評價或建議。

結論範例

　　Both city life and country life have positive and negative aspects associated with them. Choosing where to live is often not so much of a choice but rather an act of necessity. However, experiencing each of them at some point in life is definitely worth the time spent on it.

說明

1. 第一句重述主題論述。
2. 第二、三句提出自己的看法和建議。

記得你所比較或對照的東西,在文章裡所佔的比例必須是相等的。
另外這類文體中,承轉語的使用非常重要,請參考 3b-2。

5g-5 寫作練習

1. 比較家中兩位成員或學校老師,題目可以自訂,例如:**My Father and I**、**My Mother and I**、**My English Teacher and My Math Teacher** 或是 **My Two Sisters/Brothers**。

參考範文

My Father and I

My father has always had a great influence on me. Throughout my life, he has taught me many different things, and I have learned a great deal from him. Because I am his son, we share many similarities. However, as I have grown into my own person, I also have many differences from him as well.

As for visible similarities, we both have brown hair. The shape of the bones on both of our faces gives us a familial resemblance. We are nearly the same height, and we both have dark eyes. We are both in good physical shape, and we both tend to get a lot of exercise while enjoying it. The other similarities my father and I share deal with how we conduct our lives. He taught me the value of working hard, and he did it by providing himself as an example. Today, I work very hard and find satisfaction in doing so, just like he has always done. He also gave me a love of the outdoors, and we both still enjoy camping, fishing, hiking, and sailing. As well, he taught me to love classical music, and we both enjoy going to concerts whenever we are together.

Yet, I am different from my father in many ways as well. Some of my music tastes changed and were influenced by friends from my own generation. I like rock'n'roll and other types of progressive music, while he doesn't care for it. As for our professional lives, my father is a physics professor, while I chose to become a writer. Thus, I have a more artistic profession, whereas his is definitely more logical and scientific. Generally, he is also quieter and very soft-spoken, while I tend to be louder and more outgoing. I feel at home being in a large crowd of people, while he would rather be paddling his canoe out on the lake nearby our family home.

The influence that my father has had on my life has been profound. We have our differences, but the similarities in the things we both enjoy are there because he has taught them to me. Regardless of our differences, I will forever be grateful for the person he is, and the man he has taught me to be.

2. 請以 **Traditional Cards and Email Cards** 為題，比較兩者的差異性或優劣點。可以舉一些實例，讓其差異性或優劣點更清楚。

3. 請以 **The Advantages and Disadvantages of Using Cell Phones** 為題，寫一篇文章。討論使用行動電話的優缺點。

4. 請以 **A Traditional Market and a Supermarket** 為題，寫一篇文章。比較傳統市場和超級市場。

議論文
Argumentative Essays

　　議論文是運用邏輯、推理或提出證明來表明自己的態度、立場或主張。簡單地說就是說服讀者認同自己的觀點。報紙的評論就是這類文體，有時只是提出自己的見解，有時是反駁他人的觀點或作法。基本上寫議論文是一個「提出論點→運用論證方法，提出證據或理由來證明觀點→做出結論」的過程。

  5h-1 寫議論文的原則及技巧

1. 確定論點
論點一定要在引言中明確指出，構思時就要運用正反兩方的意見表 (Pro-and-Con Sheet) 選出比較具說服力的論點。

2. 證據或理由要充分而且可靠
可以列舉事實、提出數據或專家的言論，尤其是在談論一些公共議題時，更要提出很客觀的佐證。

3. 論證要合理而且邏輯嚴密
邏輯若是出錯，論點就完全不具說服力。

4. 可以提出反方論點來反駁，以增加說服力

5. 避免太強烈表示個人想法的詞語
例如避免用 I know...，改用比較委婉、公正的 In my opinion...、It seems to me that...、I would tend to believe that... 等。

6. 寫議論文通常有兩種方式：
   (1) 先提出自己贊成或反對的立場。
      提出立場之後再提出細節、列舉理由或證據來指陳看法是對的、方法是好的或呼籲的行動是可取的。
   (2) 對問題採取較客觀的態度，兼顧正反兩方。
      提出立場之後在不同的段落中從不同的角度，甚至並列正反兩方來討論，將論點以比較或對照的方式安排。把贊成與否留給讀者去決定，或者作者只在結論部分提出自己的看法。

5h-2 議論文引言的寫法

1. 若是先提出自己的立場，則主題導引要提供議題的背景資料，主題論述則需指出所討論的主題以及所持的態度。
2. 若選擇對問題兼顧正反兩方，則引言部分只需要做一般性的陳述，不需要提出自己的立場。

引言範例

以下是題目為 **Should Smoking Be Banned in Public Places?** 的引言範例。

> Secondhand smoke has recently been scientifically proven to be as much a health risk as smoking cigarettes. To protect the population from the dangers of secondhand smoke, we should make a law banning smoking in public places, specifically defined here as restaurants, bars, public transportation and anywhere people gather in public.

說明 第二句很明顯地提出立場。

5h-3　議論文主體的寫法

1. 主體就是提出證據來議論的過程

證據可以是事實、統計數字、專家說法、個人或他人的經驗。

2. 運用因果文的寫法

可以分別說明分析幾項證據，再做出造成某種結果的結論。

3. 運用比較或對照法

針對提出的事實進行對照分析，得出結論。

主體範例

　　The strongest reason for implementing smoking bans is that secondhand smoke is dangerous. Secondhand smoke is the smoke that comes off the end of a lit cigarette or is exhaled by someone smoking a cigarette. It causes the same deadly diseases in nonsmokers that smoking cigarettes causes smokers, including cancer, heart disease and high blood pressure. When nonsmokers are exposed to secondhand smoke in bars and restaurants, for example, it can take as little as 30 minutes to affect someone's body, possibly leading to a heart attack or stroke. Can you imagine going into a restaurant for dinner and having a heart attack from all the smoke?

　　People opposing smoking bans often say that in bars and restaurants, nonsmoking guests could be protected from cigarette smoke by separating smokers and nonsmokers in different sections of the restaurant or bar. This is an invalid argument because offering smoking and non-smoking sections of offices, restaurants, bars and other buildings has been proven to be ineffective. No matter how strong a building's ventilation system is, smoke will find its way into nonsmoking areas. If you can smell smoke, you're breathing smoke. Many tests done with sophisticated equipment in numerous buildings have proven that smoke will go everywhere in a building, even into the "nonsmoking" sections.

　　Another strong reason for the need for smoking bans is that workers, not just customers, must be protected from the dangers of secondhand smoke. People often forget that waiters and waitresses in bars and restaurants are exposed to lots of secondhand smoke and have nearly as much a risk of getting seriously ill from cigarette smoke. People opposed to smoking bans often say that these workers can just find jobs somewhere else. This is a poor argument, however, because you shouldn't have to change jobs just to be in a safe work environment.

說明

1. 第一段運用因果文的寫法，提出理由。
2. 第二段第一句提出反方論點，第二句之後予以反駁。第三段倒數第二句也提出反方論點，之後也予以反駁。

5h-4　議論文結論的寫法

1. 重申自己的觀點或立場，與引言相呼應。
2. 提出解決之道或應採取的行動。

結論範例

　　It is important that smoke-free policies should be enacted to prohibit smoking in areas where people gather. That way, all people are equally protected from secondhand smoke.

說明 這兩句重述立場，和引言相呼應。

5h-5　寫作練習

1. 請參考 4i-2 的參考範文 **Do We Have the Right to Use Animals in Medical Research?**，將其改寫成至少三段的文章。

提示

A. 如果採用 5h-1 所提的第一種方式，引言部分要提出自己的立場，主體部分最好能提出一個反方的論點來反駁。

B. 如果採用 5h-1 所提的第二種方式，引言部分不必提出自己的立場，只要陳述議題即可。主體部分要由正反兩方來討論。

參考範文　　　　　　　　　　　　　　　　　(以第二種方法安排要點，參見 5h-1)

Do We Have the Right to Use Animals in Medical Research?

Every year about seventeen million animals are used in laboratory experiments. However, in many countries today, people are starting to ask the difficult question: Do we human beings have the right to use animals for research?

Some people are strongly opposed to the use of animals for medical research. They believe that animals have the same right as humans do. Animals have their own right to live freely and to live without pain and fear. Human beings have no rights to let animals suffer even though humans benefit a lot from the research. They also believe that since remarkable advances have been made in biological science, it is possible to do the research by using cell culture and computer modeling instead of animals in laboratories.

Other people argue that using animals for medical research is absolutely necessary. One reason is that since it is reported that last year over twelve million animals had to be killed in animal shelters because nobody wanted them as pets, medical research is an excellent way of using these unwanted animals. What's more,

the use of animals in medical research has many practical benefits. It has enabled researchers to develop treatment for diseases such as heart diseases and depression. It would not have been possible to develop vaccines for diseases like smallpox and polio without animal research. Every drug anyone takes today was first tried on animals. Although they are treated in a cruel way, it cannot be denied that the life of a three-year-old child is more important than that of a rat.

It is clear that there are arguments against the use of animals for medical research and arguments in favor of it. The question is really difficult to answer. Maybe in the near future researchers can find better ways of doing the research, with the advance in biological science.

Vocabulary

- laboratory [`læbərə͵tɔrɪ] *n.* [C] 實驗室
- remarkable [rɪ`mɑrkəbl̩] *adj.* 卓越的
- biological [͵baɪə`lɑdʒɪkl̩] *adj.* 生物學 (上) 的

2. 你贊成中學生就讀男女合校 (co-ed schools) 或分校 (separate schools) 呢？

3. 在大多數國家裡，安樂死 (euthanasia/mercy killing) 是違法的，但有些人卻認為已無藥可醫的重症病人 (people who are terminally/incurably ill) 有權利結束自己的生命，你的看法又是如何呢？

提示

a way of helping patients with incurable diseases		
prevent dying patients from suffering unbearable pain		
in comas	suffer brain damage	depend on life machines
die with dignity	a financial burden	

■ 引言一定要有主題論述 (thesis statement) 嗎？

　　在說明文和議論文這類文體中，非常講究論點的層次結構，因此特別需要主題論述來指引讀者，甚至掌控作者文章的結構。而在敘述文和描寫文中，主題論述就沒有這麼重要了。

■ 文章 (essay) 要有幾段？可不可以只寫三段呢？

　　文章通常可分三段到八段，需依照參加的考試性質 (學科能力測驗、指定科目考試、全民英檢或托福測驗) 來決定文章的長短。另外也需視內容來決定你要寫幾段。例如第一段主題論述的句子是 "There are three advantages of sending teenage children abroad to study."，如果這三項要點可供發揮的內容夠多，就可以分三段寫。如果不夠就合成一段，這樣加上引言和結論，你就寫成了三段的作文。

■ 為什麼寫作文的時候總是想不出字來用呢?會用的大部分是國中學的字，要如何改善呢?

　　國中時所學的字彙有限，又經過反覆的練習，你當然非常熟悉。上了高中後，字彙增加很多，如果你沒有多練習，讓這些字彙不斷出現在腦海裡，它們頂多只會和你維持「點頭之交」的關係，不會是親密的朋友，寫作文時當然想不起來了。最基本的改進方法是：

1. 多閱讀，讀到優美的辭句、好的句型、有用的資料時都要反覆背誦。有朝一日寫作文時，這些存檔的字句自然泉湧而出。

2. 多寫，讓你的腦子習慣思索適當的字彙。以下兩個方法非常適合自己學習：

　　(1) 寫日記 (journal)：不一定要天天寫，也可以一週一記。如果有人可以幫你批改更好，但是沒有也無妨。就像人體有自我修復的能力一般，你還在學習英文，就像在加強身體免疫力，過一段時間後再看看自己的日記，一定會有你覺得可以修正的地方。

(2) 擴寫 (enlargement) 的練習：我們都知道作文由段落組成，段落由句子組成，句子由字組成。因此可以由最基本的造句開始練習。例如學會了一個生字 optimistic，你就可以造一個甚至兩個句意連貫的句子：I like optimistic people because they always have a bright smile on their face. However, I don't like those who are depressed all the time because they can upset people around them.。然後你就可以練習把這兩個句子擴寫成一段：

> I like optimistic people because they always have a bright smile on their face. When they are around, they always make me feel hopeful about my life. Also, they often encourage me to face the problem without feeling scared or hopeless. However, pessimistic people seldom look on the bright sight. I don't like to make friends with those who are depressed all the time because they can upset people around them.

接下來還可以更進一層，把段落擴寫成 essay。

■要寫好作文除了從這本書學到的原則及技巧之外，還有什麼平時要學習的嗎？

你還需要加強的，就是對日常生活中的所見所聞，能用心去觀察、感受、思考與想像。如此你會有比較多樣、特別的寫作材料，你的作文內容才會更豐富、更有意義。

Summary Writing
摘要寫作

▶老師通常會有一項指定作業，就是要求你把課文或假期的課外讀物寫成摘要。所謂的摘要就是把主要的內容做簡要的敘述。

6a

摘要寫作的目的

The Purpose of Summary Writing

摘要是在你把原文讀完之後，把作者的文章重點簡要地敘述出來。因此摘要寫作就有一項功能，就是檢測你是否完全瞭解文意與掌握文章主旨。這也是老師要求你寫摘要的用意之一。

6b

摘要寫作指引

Guidelines for Summary Writing

1. **仔細讀完之後，把書或文章做一份簡單的大綱。**

   這個大綱包括主旨和支持主旨的要點，但不包含次要細節，例如舉例或統計數字等可以不必納入。

2. **根據大綱寫成一個段落的摘要。**

   摘要的第一句要提出作者名或文章的篇名，並呈現出文章的主旨 (就像段落的主題句)，之後重點在作者如何支持其主旨。注意句子之間必須有連貫性。

3. **記得要用自己的文字撰寫。**

   學會運用改寫的技巧，千萬不可抄襲原作，也不可加入自己的看法或意見。

4. **摘要的長度要適中。**

   一般摘要都是原文的三分之一，而且只要一個段落 (除非有其他特別的要求)。

範例

(The Original Article)

Flash Mobs: Fun in a Flash

Over the last year, special mobs have begun appearing around the world. These mobs, however, are not protesting or meeting for political reasons. Instead, "flash mobs" have appeared for one simple reason—fun.

Flash mobs are sudden gatherings of people. Using e-mail, the Internet, and text messages, organizers contact others and tell them to go to a special place at a certain time. The people are also given instructions to act in a certain way or perform a silly activity. Then, at the location, participants in a flash mob meet, perform, and leave quickly. Most flash mobs last less than ten minutes, and many are completed in less than one minute.

The first flash mobs took place in New York City and were created by a man known only as "Bill." In June of 2003, more than one hundred people met in a department store and tried to buy one large rug for a large home they said they all shared. Another flash mob took place in a shoe store, with the participants pretending to be tourists before suddenly leaving the store, and a later flash mob happened in Central Park, with hundreds acting like birds for a short time and then disappearing.

Flash mobs quickly spread across the United States and the rest of the world. The first flash mob in Europe happened in Rome, Italy, when more than 300 people went into a store and asked for books and CDs that did not exist. Another flash mob took place in Berlin, Germany, with people taking out their cell phones and shouting, "Yes!" and then applauding before walking away.

Today, flash mobs have been reported in India, Australia, and Asia. Besides, several Websites, Web groups, and chat rooms about flash mobs have appeared.

Most participants say that they enjoy flash mobs because they are fun—and silly. In fact, one reason for the popularity of flash mobs may be that they seem to have no special reason. Because they are not serious, flash mobs provide people with comic relief in the busy and stressful modern world.

No one knows how long this craze will last. So, if you get an e-mail to take part in a flash mob, do not miss your chance. Flash mobs are popular now, but this fun and unusual fad may disappear as quickly as it appeared—in a flash!

(Summary)

In his article, "Flash Mobs: Fun in a Flash," Theodore Pigott describes flash mobs and presents the reasons for their popularity. According to him, flash mobs are events where participants gather suddenly at a moment's notice, perform a crazy activity and then leave quickly. The first flash mob was held in New York City in 2003 and this activity swiftly spreads around the world. Most flash mob members find such activities appealing not only because they are fun, but because they offer an opportunity for some excitement in their stressful daily lives. No one can predict what will happen next with flash mobs. Maybe they will die out as fast as it was born.

6c

摘要的結構

The Organization of a Summary

一般說明文和議論文的摘要可分為 Introduction、Body 和 Conclusion 這三個部分：

- **Introduction** (引言—就是這個段落的主題句)

這一部分要包含文章篇名和作者的名字，以及全文的主旨。常用的詞語有：discusses/describes the reasons...、...says/claims/suggests/shows that...。

- **Body** (主體)

這一部分要包含每一段的主旨，注意要把這些主旨以原有次序呈現。常用的詞語有 according to、...believes that... 等，若要繼續提到下一個要點，可用 goes on to say...、also reports... 等用語。

- **Conclusion** (結論句)

這一部分必須和原文的結語密切相關，而且絕不能加入個人意見。如果摘要很短，則可以不用寫結論句。常用的詞語有 concludes that...、concludes by saying that... 等。

Activity 1

讀完這篇文章之後，試著用自己的文句回答下列問題。

Bats
Jason Grenier

Imagine the face of a cute, furry animal. Did you think of a bat? Probably not. The fact is, most people think bats are downright ugly-looking. Why do you think bats look the way they do?

Most bats are nocturnal, so they're only active at night when they come out to feed. To get around in the dark, they rely on a special adaptation called echolocation. A bat makes high-pitched sounds and sends them out in pulses. The sound pulses come back as echoes that the bat can hear. The echoes let the bat know how far it is away from objects, as well as their size and shape. Since this system relies on sound, most bats have large ears that are super-sensitive. What's more, if you look at a bat's face, you will also see that many species have strange-looking growths of skin around their mouths and noses. These growths do make them look a bit like little monsters or space aliens. Actually, these growths of skin are like flaps that the bat can use to direct and control the sound pulses it sends out. This lets the bat focus on either a wide or a narrow area.

Most of the bats that use echolocation eat insects. They can locate even the smallest flying or crawling bugs in total darkness, and snatch them up. To do this, bats need to be skilful fliers. Their wings are made of leathery skin that is stretched between the fingers of each hand. That's right—bat wings are actually their hands! Besides flying, a bat can use its wings to climb or even to walk on the ground.

Yes, bats are a little bit scary looking. Some would even say they are ugly. However, the very features that make them look so scary are actually amazing adaptations that allow them to fly, hunt, and get around in the dark.

(1) What's the main idea of this article?

_____

(2) What are the three features that make bats look so ugly?

A. _____

B. _____

C. _____

(3) Write a proper concluding sentence.

Activity 2

　　請將 Activity 1 問題的答案填入下列的空格中，成為一段完整的摘要。務必要用自己的文字改寫，並加入適當的承轉語。

　　In an article entitled "Bats," Jason Grenier _____

_____ .

First, _____

because _____ .

Second, _____

because _____ .

Third, _____

because _____ .

_____

_____ .

6d
The Summary of Stories
故事的摘要

6d-1　寫故事的摘要應注意的事項

1. 要將故事在十幾個句子中做完整的摘要，需注意以下事項：
   - 首先要完全掌握故事主要情節，刪除次要情節及角色，然後濃縮成摘要，也等於是故事的大綱。
   - 其次，要有很好的運用文字的能力，把故事在摘要中說得完整而清楚。
2. 摘要一定要客觀，不可因好惡而出現自己的觀感。
3. 雖然故事可能是用過去式，但是討論它時可以用現在式。

6d-2 著名短篇小說 *The Old Man and the Sea* 的摘要

The Old Man and the Sea is a short novel by Ernest Hemingway. It is about an old Cuban fisherman, Santiago. Every morning he rows his skiff out into the Gulf Stream, but every evening he comes back without a single fish. At first a young boy shares his bad luck. But one day the boy is forced to leave by his father. On the eighty-fiftieth day, he rows out of the harbor into the gulf alone. Around noon, a marlin starts nibbling at the bait. It is the biggest marlin ever seen in those waters. He struggles with the giant fish for two days and nights. Almost exhausted, he finally kills it, two feet longer than the boat. Lashing the fish to his boat, he sails for home, hoping that he will make a fortune. Soon sharks come to attack his catch. Alone and exhausted by the struggle, he is forced to lose the battle with the sharks. The sharks leave him nothing but the skeleton. With it, he returns to Havana Harbor. The other fishermen gather around and marvel at his courage and endurance.

Activity

請任選讀過的課外讀物或者最近看的影片，寫成 150～200 字的摘要。

■英文作文中常見的文法錯誤一

㈠ 詞性的混淆

　　錯誤的句子

1. She cannot choice between the two lovers.   4. My grandfather dead ten years ago.

1. She cannot choice between the   4. My grandfather dead ten years ago.
　 two lovers.   5. He successed as a fashion designer.
2. We eager to learn.   6. I against death penalty.
3. Healthy is important.   7. Help others will make me happy.

　　改正後的句子

　　1. She cannot **choose** between the two lovers.

　　　　→ choice 是名詞，在 cannot 之後要用動詞 choose。

　　2. We **are eager** to learn. → eager 是形容詞。

　　3. **Health** is important. → healthy 是形容詞，主詞要用名詞 health。

　　4. My grandfather **died** ten years ago. → dead 是形容詞。

　　5. He **succeeded** as a fashion designer. → success 是名詞。

　　6. I **am** against death penalty. → against 是介系詞。

　　7. **Helping** others will make me happy.

　　　　→ help 是動詞，不能當作主詞，要加上 "-ing" 變成動名詞。

㈡ 動詞的時態與及物或不及物

　　錯誤的句子

A. 時態

　　1. She threw herself back and stand staring at the wall.

　　2. When she was young, she often goes jogging in the evening.

　　3. Miss Li is our English teacher. She teaches English for 30 years.

B. 及物或不及物動詞

　　4. The meeting was over when she arrived the office.

　　5. No man can serve for two masters.

　　6. He insisted telling her the truth.

改正後的句子

A. 時態

1. She threw herself back and **stood** staring at the wall.

   → stand 必須與 threw 一樣都用過去式。

2. When she was young, she often **went** jogging in the evening.

   → 由 when 子句的動詞 was 得知時間是過去，所以要用過去式 went。

3. Miss Li is our English teacher. She **has been teaching** English for 30 years.

   →由過去某時延續到現在，而且還在進行中的動作，用現在完成進行式。

B. 及物或不及物動詞

4. The meeting was over when she arrived **at** the office.

   → arrive 是不及物動詞（arrive at/in + 地方）。

5. No man can **serve** two masters. → serve 是及物動詞，不需再加介係詞 for。

6. He **insisted on** telling her the truth.

   → insist 是不及物動詞，要加介系詞 on 才能接受詞，但若要接子句，則不需加上 on，可直接以 "insist that..." 的方式呈現。

㈢ 名詞的單複數

錯誤的句子

1. That would be a bad news.
2. I helped her with her homeworks.
3. Every students in the classroom knows the answer.

改正後的句子

1. That would be **bad news**. → news 是不可數名詞。

2. I helped her with her **homework**. → homework 是不可數名詞。

3. **Every student** in the classroom knows the answer.

   → every 之後要接單數名詞。

Personal Letters
私人信函

▶書信是一種簡單的寫作方式。本章元要介紹的是一般比較常使用的私人信函,包含朋友間的問候函、生日卡、感謝卡等。

7a　信件
Letters

　　也稱做 informal letters,是寫給家人和朋友以聯絡彼此感情、表達感謝或祝賀、分享彼此的生活或工作內容等的信函。

7a-1　私人信件的格式

　　一般英文的非正式信件分為以下五個部分:

1. 信頭 (Heading)

在信件的右上角,包括寄件人地址和日期,有些私人信件可以只寫日期。

> No. 100, Ln. 80,
> Jongshan Rd. Sec. 2
> Taipei, Taiwan 112
> May 10, 2006

(美國日期的寫法是月、日、年的順序;而英國為日、月、年,例如:10 May, 2006)

2. 稱謂 (Salutation)

稱謂之後要加逗點,另外要視彼此的關係決定如何稱呼,對於不熟識的朋友或長輩,稱謂要用較正式的 "Dear Mr. Smith,"、"Dear Miss Clinton," 等。對於自己的晚輩、朋友或是親人則可直呼其名,例如:"Dear David,"、"Dear Iris,"、"Dear Mom,"、"Dear Uncle Ted," 或 "My Dear Uncle," 等。

3. 信文 (Body)

通常包含問候語、內容和結尾三部分。

・問候語：此部分為寒暄問候之類的用語，例如：

　　How is everything at school?　　It's been a long time since we last met.

・內容：此部分主要是傳達寫信的目的、談自己的課業、家庭或工作情況。

・結尾：此部分和開頭一樣盡量簡短，例如：

　　Keep in touch.　　Hoping to hear from you soon.

　　Write soon and tell us how you are doing.

　　Please give my best wishes to your family.

4. 結尾辭 (Closing)

結尾辭之後要加逗點 (例如 "Sincerely Yours,")，這部分類似中文書信結尾的「謹上」，對一般朋友用的是 "Sincerely Yours,"、"Sincerely," 或 "Yours Truly,"，而比較親密的朋友用的是 "Your friend,"、"Love,"、"With love,"、"Best wishes," 或 "Best regards,"。

5. 簽名 (Signature)

通常位於結尾辭下方，與結尾辭齊頭。

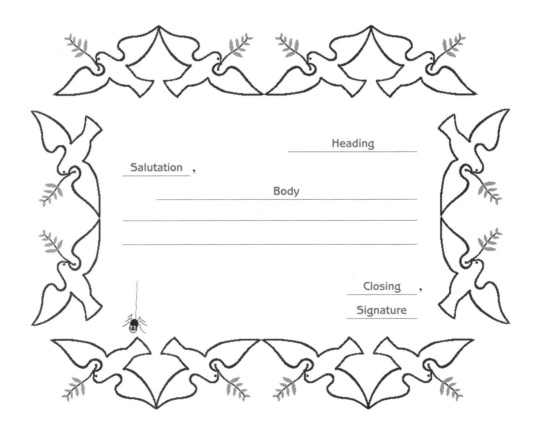

7a-2 信件的範例

August 20, 2002

Dear Rosette,

Hi! How is your "new life"? We are glad to know that you like your new apartment. It's a great joy to live there, isn't it? You don't have to care too much about your roommates anymore.

Everything here is O.K. Don't worry about us. Iris is going to attend National Taiwan University next month. Jasper is so busy doing the research that he can't afford to get exercise. He is gaining weight. I'm afraid that he is going to have a "beer belly." Jane still can't walk well with her sprained ankle. We're hoping that she can go hiking with us when you come to visit us next month. We've been looking forward to seeing you soon.

With love,
Grace

7a-3 信封的範例

寄件人姓名地址
↑

Mei-hua Lin
6 F, No. 100, Lane 80, Wen-lin N. Rd.
Peitou, Taipei 112
Taiwan, R.O.C.

Express Mail

Miss Janice Fritz
3060 Edwin Ave.
Fortlee, NJ 07024
U.S.A.

Do Not Fold

↓
收件人姓名地址

說明

1. (1) 英文地址是由小單位寫到大單位，與中文地址相反。例如地址是中華民國臺灣臺北市 11262 北投區承德路七段六巷十二弄八號六樓，英文寫成：

    6F, No. 8, Alley 12, Lane 6, Cheng-te Rd., Sec. 7

    Taipei, 11262

    Taiwan, R.O.C.

   (2) 臺灣的郵遞區號寫在城市之後，而美加地區郵遞區號則寫在州名或省名之後。例如：

    4670 Albany Circle #106　　　　1500 Austin Ave.

    San Jose, C.A. 95129　　　　　Vancouver, B.C. V7C5M

    U.S.A.　　　　　　　　　　　Canada

   (3) 住址中常用的單字及其簡寫：

室　Room/Rm.	大道　Boulevard/Boul.
樓　Floor/F.	大街　Avenue/Ave.
弄　Alley/Aly.	區　District/Dist.
巷　Lane/Ln.	鎮　Town
段　Section/Sec.	鄉　Township
街　Street/St.	村　Village
路　Road/Rd.	縣　County

2. 上面的範例中，郵票下方寫的是郵寄方式，例如：

   Air Mail　航空信　　　　　Express Mail　快遞

   Registered　掛號信　　　　Printed Matter　印刷品

3. 上頁的範例中，左下角為要請收件人注意的事項，畫上底線以作為強調。例如：

   Do Not Fold 請勿折疊　　　Photo Inside/Photo Enclosed 內附照片

Activity

寫一封信給朋友或親人敘述你的近況，並寫好信封。

Cards
卡片

7b-1 卡片的格式

卡片的格式和信件大致是相同的。一般有特定目的的卡片，都會寫一些特定的祝福語。例如以 May 或 Wish 開頭的祈願句：

> May you have a wonderful holiday.   Wish you a Merry Christmas!

7b-2 卡片的範例

1. Christmas card

Dec. 5, 2006

Dear Iris,

It's the first time you spend Christmas in Manhattan. You must be looking forward to it. May you have a joyful holiday. Remember to tell us how you feel when you watch the ball drop in Times Square on New Year's Eve.

Love,
Grace

2. Birthday card

Happy Birthday!!

Dear Joyce,

What a special day! I can remember how we celebrated each other's birthday when you were in Taiwan. They were all wonderful memories. Take care and Happy Birthday!!

With love,
Jane

3. **Thank-you card**

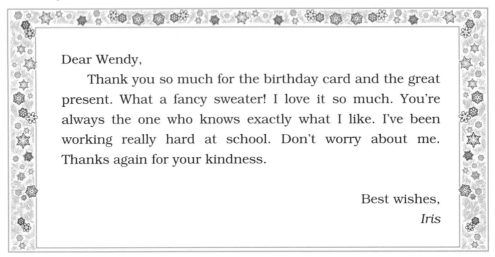

Dear Wendy,

   Thank you so much for the birthday card and the great present. What a fancy sweater! I love it so much. You're always the one who knows exactly what I like. I've been working really hard at school. Don't worry about me. Thanks again for your kindness.

                                           Best wishes,
                                                    Iris

Activity

寫一張謝卡給朋友，感謝他或她對你的關懷。

■英文作文中常見的文法錯誤二

㈣ Sentence Fragments（句子片斷）

改正後的句子

錯誤的句子

1. I'll stand by you. As long as you decide to make a fresh start.
2. I care very much about how I look. Because it matters.
3. Don't be in a hurry. You step by step.
4. Hated him, but she still took care of him.

改正後的句子

1. I'll stand by you **as long as** you decide to make a fresh start.
   → as long as...子句是從屬子句，必須要加上主要子句才是完整的句子，否則只是 sentence fragment。

2. I care very much about how I look **because** it matters.
   → because...子句也是從屬子句，必須加上主要子句才是完整的句子。

3. Don't be in a hurry. You **can go** step by step.
   → step by step 不是動詞，少了動詞也是 sentence fragment。

4. **She** hated him, but she still took care of him.
   → hated him 少了主詞，也是 sentence fragment。

㈤ Run on Sentences（連綴句）

錯誤的句子

1. Her foot touched something soft, she turned and looked down.
2. My hair is curly and soft, I usually keep it braided.
3. Many customers are cat-lovers, they come to play with the cats.
4. She hated him, she still took good care of him.

改正後的句子

1. Her foot touched something soft**.** She turned and looked down.
   → 用句號把它分成兩句。

2. My hair is curly and soft, **but** I usually keep it braided.

    → 用對等連接詞 but 來連接兩句。

3. Many customers are cat-lovers, **who** come to play with the cats.

    → 用關係代名詞 who 的非限定用法，把兩句連接起來。

4. **Although** she hated him, she still took good care of him.

    → 用從屬連接詞 although 來連接兩句。

㈥ 以中文的詞序或字義「對號入座」

  錯誤的句子

1. 你必須去理髮。

   You must to get your hair cut.

2. 時光是不復返的。

   Time is never returns.

3. 你沒來參加我的宴會真的是很遺憾。

   You didn't come to my party is a pity.

4. 不管你同意與否，我都要去買那棟房子。

   No matter you agree or not, I am going to buy the house.

5. 雖然恨他，但是她還是把他照顧得很好。

   Although she hated him, but she still took good care of him.

6. 再用功一點，我考試就可以考好。

   Study harder, and I'll do well on the exam.

7. 有時候憂慮讓我不能好好睡一覺。

   Sometimes worry makes me cannot have a good sleep.

8. 有一盞燈和一個 CD 唱盤在桌上。

   There have a lamp and a CD player on the desk.

9. 有四個孩子在結冰的湖面上溜冰。

   There are four kids skated on the frozen lake.

改正後的句子

1. You **must get** your hair cut.

    → must 是助動詞，之後不可接 to + V, 要接原形動詞。

2. Time **never** returns.

   → 中文的「是」可以和動詞一起出現，但英文的 Be 動詞也是動詞，這裡只需要 return 一個動詞。

3. **That** you didn't come to my party is a pity.

   It's a pity that you didn't come to my party.

   → 以 that 子句 (名詞子句) 作主詞或用虛主詞 It... 的句型。

4. **Whether** you agree **or not**, I am going to buy the house.

   → 中文的「不論或不管…與否」，在英文是 whether...or not。

5. **Although** she hated him, she still took good care of him.

   → although 是從屬連接詞，but 是對等連接詞，兩個子句合併只需要一個連接詞。

6. Study harder, and **you'll** do well on the exam.

   → 祈使句省略的主詞是 you，所以 I'll 要改為 you'll。另外如果主詞要維持第一人稱，原本的祈使句就要改成一個從屬子句 (**If I** study harder, I'll do well on the exam.)。

7. Sometimes worry **makes it impossible for me to** have a good sleep.

   → cannot have a good sleep 不能當作 make 的受詞補語。

8. There **are** a lamp and a CD player on the desk.

   → 沒有 there have 的說法。

9. There are four kids **skating** on the frozen lake.

   → are 就是動詞，不可再有另一個動詞 skated 在一個句子裡，應該要用分詞片語 skating 去修飾 kids。

建議 如果你覺得這些錯誤的句子讀起來很順，就要提高警覺了，因為你好像在用中文的邏輯寫英文句子。句子結構正確是寫作的基本條件。

KEY

Chapter 1

1a

- **Activity 1** 參考答案

  Who were the old couple in the car?

  What were they saying?　　　　　　　Where were they leaving for?

  What was the bad guy doing?

  Why was he pointing his knife at the old man?

  How did the old couple feel with the bad guy in their car?

  How did old couple save themselves?　　Where did they stop their car?

- **Activity 2** 參考答案

  cell phones
  - convenient → call anywhere
  - magnetic waves → brain cancer
  - troubles
    - too dependent on them → spend a lot more money
    - lose private life → can be reached everywhere

- **Activity 3** 參考答案

Numbers	Gifts	New Year's Day	Ghost Month
4	clock	sweep the floor	move to a new house
6	handkerchief	break a bowl	redecorate a house
8	umbrella	fish	wedding
	fan	red	buy a new car

1b

- **Activity 1** 參考答案

  (Topic Sentence: People are aware of the troubles cell phones cause.)

  Point 1: magnetic waves—brain cancer

  Point 2: too dependent on cell phones—spend a lot of money

  Point 3: lose private life—can be reached everywhere

  (Concluding sentence: Once people are too much dependent on cell phones, they cannot avoid getting into these troubles.)

· **Activity 2** 參考答案

Topic sentence: My mother is my favorite family member.

Point 1: a great listener

  a. listen and laugh with me

  b. listen and then give guidance

Point 2: respect my decision

  a. let me decide what I want to be

  b. respect my decision on which school to go to

Point 3: a positive philosophy of life

  a. see the bright side of things

  b. ready to share joy with others

Concluding sentence: These are the reasons why among my family members
I like my mother best.

Chapter 2

2b

· **Activity 1**

(2) (Idioms) can reveal some of the culture behind a language.

(3) (Bats) perform an important ecological function throughout the world.

(4) It's easy to form (bad eating habits).

(5) (Nutritionists) have made several recommendations to help teenagers
control their weight.

· **Activity 2**

(1) a、只有主題，缺乏主題論述，沒有討論的方向。

(2) a、語意太模糊。

(3) a、呈現的只是一個事實，缺乏討論空間。

(4) b、不夠清楚，語意模糊。

· **Activity 3**

(1) The kitten sends messages through its whiskers.

(2) A well-trained kitten knows that it must not steal food.

(3) The Earth has warmed about 1 degree Fahrenheit in the last 100 years—
more in some places, like the Arctic.

(4) There are two main sources that help the English language to remain alive and in use in the United States.

- **Activity 4**

    (1) A. b   B. b   C. b   D. c

    (2) A. Cards now are different from they used to be.

    B. Trekking in high mountains is dangerous, so we must be well-prepared.

    C. Hiccups occur when your diaphragm is disturbed for some reason.

    D. Many things can cause hiccups.

    (3) A. I like rainy days, especially in spring.

    B. Spring is full of life and hope.

    C. My trip in Nepal was extremely terrible because I sprained my ankle there.

2c

- **Activity 1**

    (2) 123   (3) 231   (4) 231   (5) 312   (6) 213   (7) 132   (8) 132

- **Activity 2** 參考答案

    (1) My heart was beating fast, and my hands were sweating. What's more, I could hardly utter a word.

    (2) She offers help whenever her friends are in need. She will do everything possible to help them get out of trouble.

    (3) She always talks with her mouth full of food. She likes to put her arms and elbows on the table while eating.

    (4) Every Saturday we go mountain climbing in Yangmingshan. On Sundays, we like to go to Peitou to soak in hot springs to relax.

    (5) We usually help her to wash dishes, take out the garbage, do the laundry, clean our own room and bathroom, and walk our dog. When we have done a good job, she will reward us by giving us a snack or warm hug.

    (6) His feelings often change swiftly. In the morning he is happy, but in the afternoon he may be sad and depressed.

- **Activity 3**

    (1) A. 第二句是主題句。

B. 作者提出細節來說明 certain qualities。

C. 以 "One.... Another.... Besides...." 舉出了三項 qualities。

(2) A. 舉例提出統計數據和說明因果。

　　B. 舉出這些數字是為了證明禽流感造成很大的損害。

　　C. 最後一句說明結果，前一句提出因。

(3) A. 第一句是主題句。

　　B. 運用舉例和對照的技巧。

　　C. 第六句針對第五句提出更具體明確的說明。

(4) A. 第一句是主題句。

　　B. 提出細節和因果關係說明造成的問題。

　　C. 總共是五個方面。第一個是侵略了珍貴的農地，第二個是在草地築土堆，第三個為掠奪果樹，第四個為攻擊電器，第五個則為他們的螫針可能會讓家畜或人類致命。

　　D. 這兩句是互為因果的關係，be attracted to electromagnetic fields 是因，造成 attack electrical insulation or wire connections 這個果；而這個果又造成了下一句的 electrical shorts, fires, and other damage to electrical equipment。

- **Activity 4**

　無標準答案

2d

- **Activity**

　(1) Understanding what your body really needs is the key to well-being.

　(2) If you have a positive attitude, it can help you achieve your dreams and succeed in living a truly fulfilling life.

　(3) No wonder more and more companies are allowing their office workers to wear casual clothes to work.

Chapter 3

3a

- **Activity 1**

　(1) 缺少一致性，根據主題句可得知主題為 Christopher Reeve 是永遠的 Superman，段落應該要說明理由，也就是傷後如何奮鬥，但第三句跟主題無關，第七句之後又偏離了主題。

(2) 具有一致性，因為一整段都只有一個主題，就是 Reeve 對英雄的看法。

- **Activity 2**

    (1) He is a college student.

    (2) Many schools offer children athletic programs.

    (3) Almost all the people in English-speaking countries know the song. I like the song very much. Like us, people in Scotland are superstitious.

    (4) Most flash mobs last less than ten minutes, and many are completed in less than one minute.

3b

- **Activity 1**

    (1) A. 按照時間次序說明紅茶的製作過程。

      B. then、next 和 finally。

    (2) A. from general to specific 的邏輯關係。

      B. 先談果後談因的邏輯關係。

      C. 先談因後談果的邏輯關係。

- **Activity 2**

    (1) BA   (2) AB   (3) CAB   (4) BCA   (5) ACB

- **Activity 3**

    (1) A. In contrast   B. For instance/example   C. Therefore

    (2) A. also   B. first   C. then   D. For instance/example

    (3) A. but   B. Because   C. In addition   D. In fact

- **Activity 4**

    (1) C   (2) B   (3) B   (4) C   (5) C   (6) C

- **Activity 5**

    (1) FAD   (2) ECB

Exercises

I. 1. CDAB   2. ACBD   3. CADB   4. DBAC

II. (以下答案僅供參考)

1.

Tattoos had several purposes. The most popular reason for getting a tattoo was for decoration. Tattoos were also used to identify different tribes or groups. Sometimes they were used to show that a child had become an adult.

Moreover, sailors liked to get tattoos as souvenirs of the places they had visited.

2.

Social attitudes about tattoos have changed. People with tattoos are no longer seen as criminals or troublemakers. In fact, tattoos have become so common among movie stars and pop singers that it is hard to think of a famous person without one. Besides, more and more average people are getting tattoos, including mothers and even grandmothers.

3.

A healthy breakfast gives children an advantage in life. Scientific studies have proved that children who eat a healthy breakfast concentrate better at school, and (they) are less likely to misbehave or miss classes. In addition, children that eat breakfast generally do not overeat in the day. Consequently, they are less likely to develop obesity.

4.

Helen Keller was born a healthy baby in 1880. However, at 18 months, she suffered an illness that caused her to lose her sight and her hearing. Helen was raised almost like a caged beast with no discipline or education, because no one could communicate with her. When Helen was six, her parents hired Annie Sullivan, a twenty-year-old teacher who had been blind herself, to teach Helen.

Chapter 4
本章沒有標準答案，請自行做寫作練習。

Chapter 5
本章沒有標準答案，請自行做寫作練習。

Chapter 6
6c

· **Activity 1** 參考答案

  (1) The article describes three features that make bats ugly.

  (2) A. Bats have large ears.

B. Bats have growths of skin around their mouths and noses.

C. Bats have hand-like wings made of skin stretched between their fingers.

(3) In order to locate their prey and navigate around in the dark, bats have large ears, strange-looking skin, and hand-like wings; as a result, they look like monsters.

- **Activity 2** 參考答案

　　In an article entitled "Bats," Jason Grenier describes three features that make bats ugly. First, bats have large ears because they need to pick up the echo reflected after they emit high-pitched pulses. Second, they have growths of skin around their mouths and noses because these growths help them to gain control in the echolocation. Third, their hand-like wings are made of leathery skin stretched between their fingers, because they need to be fast fliers to catch insects or bugs easily. In order to locate their prey and navigate around in the dark, bats have large ears, strange-looking skin, and hand-like wings; as a result, they look like monsters.

6d

- **Activity**

無標準答案

Chapter 7

7a

- **Activity** 參考答案

Dear Emily,

　　I am OK with my new life and job. I have been a little busy with two projects. I just finished one and shipped the whole piece to system test group. My colleagues began to work on another new one two weeks ago and I am a little behind schedule.

　　This is the coldest and longest winter in the past 20 years here. We've had 7 snows up to now. There're all kinds of snow: dry as powder, clear as crystal, light as feather, or wet and heavy as mud. My brother and I shoveled 2 feet depth snow away from the driveway. It took us 2 or more hours to finish the work. What an exercise! I don't know about other people, but I've really had enough of winter.

I'd like to be back to Taipei this summer if it is possible.

Love,
Grace

7b

- **Activity** 參考答案

Dear Jasmine,

I would like to thank you for being such a wonderful friend. When I feel frustrated, you are always the first one to comfort me and offer help. It is your friendship that makes me feel life is beautiful and worth living.

Yours always,
Janice

基礎英文法養成篇

英文學很久，文法還是囧？
本書助你釐清「觀念」、抓對「重點」、舉一反三「練習」，
不用砍掉重練，也能無縫接軌、輕鬆養成英文法！

陳曉菁　編著

特色一： **條列章節重點**
每章節精選普高技高必備文法重點，編排環環相扣、循序漸進。

特色二： **學習重點圖像化與表格化**
將觀念與例句以圖表統整，視覺化學習組織概念，輕鬆駕馭文法重點。

特色三： **想像力學文法很不一樣**
將時態比喻為「河流」，假設語氣比喻為「時光機」，顛覆枯燥文法印象。

特色四： **全面補給一次到位**
「文法小精靈」適時補充說明，「文法傳送門」提供相關文法知識章節，
觸類旁通學習更全面。

特色五： **即時練習Level up!**
依據文法重點設計多元題型，透過練習釐清觀念，融會貫通熟練文法。

跨閱英文

王信雲 編著　　車昀庭 審定

學習不限於書本上的知識，而是「跨」出去，學習帶得走的能力！

跨文化
呈現不同的國家或文化，進而了解及尊重多元文化。

跨世代
橫跨時間軸，經歷不同的世代，見證其發展里程碑。

跨領域
整合兩個或兩個以上領域之間的知識，拓展知識領域。

1. 以新課綱的核心素養為主軸
網羅 3 大面向──「跨文化」、「跨世代」、「跨領域」，共 24 篇文章，引發你對各項議題的好奇。包含多元文化、家庭、生涯規劃、科技、資訊、性別平等、生命、閱讀素養、戶外、環境、海洋、防災等之多項重要議題，開拓多元領域的視野！

2. 跨出一板一眼的作答舒適圈
以循序漸進的實戰演練，搭配全彩的圖像設計，引導學生跳脫形式學習，練出「混合題型」新手感，並更進一步利用「進階練習」的訓練，達到整合知識和活用英文的能力。最後搭配「延伸活動」，讓你在各式各樣的活動中 *FUN* 學英文！

3. 隨書附贈活動式設計解析本
自學教學兩相宜，方便你完整對照中譯，有效理解文章，並有詳細的試題解析，讓你擊破各個答題關卡，從容應試每一關！

Intermediate Reading:

英文閱讀 High Five

掌握大考新趨勢，搶先練習新題型！

王隆興 編著

★全書分為 5 大主題：生態物種、人文歷史、科學科技、環境保育、醫學保健，共 50 篇由外籍作者精心編寫之文章。

★題目仿 111 學年度學測參考試卷命題方向設計，為未來大考提前作準備，搶先練習第二部分新題型──混合題。

★隨書附贈解析夾冊，方便練習後閱讀文章中譯及試題解析，並於解析補充每回文章精選的 15 個字彙。